Other books by Anatole France:

Thaïs
Penguin Island
The White Stone
Dieux Ont Soif
The Revolt of the Angels
Mother of Pearl
The Gods Will Have Blood
The Red Lily
Livre de Mon AMI
The Crime of Sylvestre Bonnard
Jardin D'epicure
The Human Tragedy

THAÏS

Anatole France
translated by Robert B. Douglas

WILDSIDE PRESS
Doylestown, Pennsylvania

First published in 1909.

Thaïs
A publication of
WILDSIDE PRESS
P.O. Box 301
Holicong, PA 18928-0301

www.wildsidepress.com

PART
THE FIRST

The Lotus

In those days there were many hermits living in the desert. On both banks of the Nile numerous huts, built by these solitary dwellers, of branches held together by clay, were scattered at a little distance from each other, so that the inhabitants could live alone, and yet help one another in case of need. Churches, each surmounted by a cross, stood here and there amongst the huts, and the monks flocked to them at each festival to celebrate the services or to partake of the Communion. There were also, here and there on the banks of the river, monasteries, where the cenobites lived in separate cells, and only met together that they might the better enjoy their solitude.

Both hermits and cenobites led abstemious lives, taking no food till after sunset, and eating nothing but bread with a little salt and hyssop. Some retired into the desert, and led a still more strange life in some cave or tomb.

All lived in temperance and chastity; they wore a hair shirt and a hood, slept on the bare ground after long watching, prayed, sang psalms, and, in short, spent their days in works of penitence. As an atonement for original sin, they refused their body not only all pleasures and satisfactions, but even that care and attention which in this age are deemed indispensable. They believed that the diseases of our members purify our souls, and the flesh could put on no adornment more glorious than wounds and ulcers. Thus, they thought they fulfilled the words of the prophet, "The desert shall rejoice and blossom as the rose."

Amongst the inhabitants of the holy Thebaid, there were some who passed their days in asceticism and contemplation; others gained their livelihood by plaiting palm fiber, or by working at harvest-time for the neighboring farmers. The Gentiles wrongly suspected some of them of living by brigandage, and allying themselves to the nomadic Arabs who robbed the caravans. But, as a matter of fact, the monks despised riches, and the odor of their sanctity rose to heaven.

Angels in the likeness of young men came, staff in hand, as travelers, to visit the hermitages; whilst demons — having assumed the form of Ethiopians or of animals — wandered round the habitations of the hermits in order to lead them into temptation. When the monks went in the morning to fill their pitcher at the spring, they saw the footprints of Satyrs and Aigipans in the sand. The Thebaid was, really and spiritually, a battlefield, where, at all times, and more especially at night, there were terrible conflicts between heaven and hell.

The ascetics, furiously assailed by legions of the damned, defended themselves — with the help of God and the angels — by fasting, prayer, and penance. Sometimes carnal desires pricked them so cruelly that they cried aloud with pain, and their lamentations rose to the starlit heavens mingled with the howls of the hungry hyænas. Then it was that the demons appeared in delightful forms. For though the demons are, in reality, hideous, they sometimes assume an appearance of beauty which prevents their real nature from being recognized. The ascetics of the Thebaid were amazed to see in their cells phantasms of delights unknown even to the voluptuaries of the age. But, as they were under the sign of the Cross, they did not succumb to these temptations, and the unclean spirits, assuming again their true character, fled at daybreak, filled with rage and shame. It was not unusual to meet at dawn one of these beings, flying away and weeping, and replying to those who questioned it, "I weep and groan because one of the Christians who live here has beaten me with rods, and driven me away in ignominy."

The power of the old saints of the desert extended over all sinners and unbelievers. Their goodness was sometimes terrible. They derived from the Apostles authority to punish all offences against the true and only God, and no earthly power could save those they condemned. Strange tales were told in the cities, and even as far as Alexandria, how the earth had opened and swallowed up certain wicked persons whom one of these saints struck with his staff. Therefore they were feared by all evil-doers, and particularly by mimes, mountebanks, married priests, and prostitutes.

Such was the sanctity of these holy men that even wild beasts felt their power. When a hermit was about to die, a lion came and dug a grave with its claws. The saint knew by this that God had called him, and he went and kissed all his brethren on the cheek. Then he lay down joyfully, and slept in the Lord.

Now that Anthony, who was more than a hundred years old, had retired to Mount Colzin with his well-beloved disciples, Macarius and Amathas, there was no monk in the Thebaid more renowned for good works than Paphnutius, the Abbot of Antinoë. Ephrem and Serapion had a greater number of followers, and in the spiritual and temporal management of their monasteries surpassed him. But Paphnutius observed the most rigorous fasts, and often went for three entire days without taking food. He wore a very rough hair shirt, he flogged himself night and morning, and lay for hours with his face to the earth.

His twenty-four disciples had built their huts near his, and imitated his austerities. He loved them all dearly in Jesus Christ, and unceasingly exhorted them to good works. Amongst his spiritual children were men who had been robbers for many years, and had been persuaded by the exhortations of the holy abbot to embrace the monastic life, and who now edified their companions by the purity of their lives. One, who had been cook to the Queen of Abyssinia, and was converted by the Abbot of Antinoë, never ceased to weep. There was also Flavian, the deacon, who knew the Scriptures, and spoke well; but the disciple of Paphnutius who surpassed all the others in holiness was a young peasant named Paul, and surnamed the Fool, because of his extreme simplicity. Men laughed at his childishness, but God favored him with visions, and by bestowing upon him the gift of prophecy.

Paphnutius passed his life in teaching his disciples, and in ascetic practices. Often did he meditate upon the Holy Scriptures in order to find allegories in them. Therefore he abounded in good works, though still young. The devils, who so rudely assailed the good hermits, did not dare to approach him. At night, seven little jackals sat in the moonlight in front of his cell, silent and motionless, and with their ears pricked up. It was believed that they were seven devils, who, owing to his sanctity, could not cross his threshold.

Paphnutius was born at Alexandria of noble parents, who had instructed him in all profane learning. He had even been allured by the falsehoods of the poets, and in his early youth had been misguided enough to believe that the human race had all been drowned by a deluge in the days of Deucalion, and had argued with his fellow scholars concerning the nature, the attributes, and even the existence of God. He then led a life of dissipation, after the manner of the Gentiles, and he recalled the memory of those days with shame and horror.

"At that time," he used to say to the brethren, "I seethed in the cauldron of false delights."

He meant by that that he had eaten food properly dressed, and frequented the public baths. In fact, until his twentieth year he had continued to lead the ordinary existence of those times, which now seemed to him rather death than life; but, owing to the lessons of the priest Macrinus, he then became a new man.

The truth penetrated him through and through, and — as he used to say — entered his soul like a sword. He embraced the faith of Calvary, and worshipped Christ crucified. After his baptism he remained yet a year amongst the Gentiles, unable to cast off the bonds of old habits. But one day he entered a church, and heard a deacon read from the Bible, the verse, "If thou wilt be perfect, go and sell that thou hast, and give to the poor." Thereupon he sold all that he had, gave away the money in alms, and embraced the monastic life.

During the ten years that he had lived remote from men, he no longer seethed in the cauldron of false delights, but more profitably macerated his flesh in the balms of penitence.

One day when, according to his pious custom, he was recalling to mind the hours he had lived apart from God, and examining his sins one by one, that he might the better ponder on their enormity, he remembered that he had seen at the theatre at Alexandria a very beautiful actress named Thaïs. This woman showed herself in the public games, and did not scruple to perform dances, the movements of which, arranged only too cleverly, brought to mind the most horrible passions. Sometimes she imitated the horrible deeds

which the Pagan fables ascribe to Venus, Leda, or
Pasiphaë. Thus she fired all the spectators with lust,
and when handsome young men, or rich old ones,
came, inspired with love, to hang wreaths of flowers
round her door, she welcomed them, and gave herself
up to them. So that, whilst she lost her own soul, she
also ruined the souls of many others.

She had almost led Paphnutius himself into the sins
of the flesh. She had awakened desire in him, and he
had once approached the house of Thaïs. But he
stopped on the threshold of the courtesan's house,
partly restrained by the natural timidity of extreme
youth — he was then but fifteen years old — and partly
by the fear of being refused on account of his want of
money, for his parents took care that he should commit no great extravagances.

God, in His mercy, had used these two means to
prevent him from committing a great sin. But Paphnutius had not been grateful to Him for that, because
at that time he was blind to his own interests, and did
not know that he was lusting after false delights. Now,
kneeling in his cell, before the image of that holy cross
on which hung, as in a balance, the ransom of the
world, Paphnutius began to think of Thaïs, because
Thaïs was a sin to him, and he meditated long, according to ascetic rules, on the fearful hideousness of the
carnal delights with which this woman had inspired
him in the days of his sin and ignorance. After some
hours of meditation the image of Thaïs appeared to
him clearly and distinctly. He saw her again, as he had
seen her when she tempted him, in all the beauty of
the flesh. At first she showed herself like a Leda, softly
lying upon a bed of hyacinths, her head bowed, her
eyes humid and filled with a strange light, her nostrils
quivering, her mouth half open, her breasts like two
flowers, and her arms smooth and fresh as two brooks.
At this sight Paphnutius struck his breast and said —

"I call Thee to witness, my God, that I have considered how heinous has been my sin."

Gradually the face of the image changed its expression. Little by little the lips of Thaïs, by lowering at the corners of the mouth, expressed a mysterious suffering. Her large eyes were filled with tears and lights; her breast heaved with sighs, like the sighing of a wind that precedes a tempest. At this sight Paphnutius was troubled to the bottom of his soul. Prostrating himself on the floor, he uttered this prayer —

"Thou who hast put pity in our hearts, like the morning dew upon the fields, O just and merciful God, be Thou blessed! Praise! praise be unto Thee! Put away from Thy servant that false tenderness which tempts to concupiscence, and grant that I may only love Thy creatures in Thee, for they pass away, but Thou endurest for ever. If I care for this woman, it is only because she is Thy handiwork. The angels themselves feel pity for her. Is she not, O Lord, the breath of Thy mouth? Let her not continue to sin with many citizens and strangers. There is great pity for her in my heart. Her wickednesses are abominable, and but to think of them makes my flesh creep. But the more wicked she is, the more do I lament for her. I weep when I think that the devils will torment her to all eternity."

As he was meditating in this way, he saw a little jackal lying at his feet. He felt much surprised, for the door of his cell had been closed since the morning. The animal seemed to read the Abbot's thoughts, and wagged its tail like a dog. Paphnutius made the sign of the cross and the beast vanished. He knew then that, for the first time, the devil had entered his cell, and he uttered a short prayer; then he thought again about Thaïs.

"With God's help," he said to himself, "I must save her." And he slept.

The next morning, when he had said his prayers, he

went to see the sainted Palemon, a holy hermit who lived some distance away. He found him smiling quietly as he dug the ground, as was his custom. Palemon was an old man, and cultivated a little garden; the wild beasts came and licked his hands, and the devils never tormented him.

"May God be praised, brother Paphnutius," he said, as he leaned upon his spade.

"God be praised!" replied Paphnutius. "And peace be unto my brother."

"The like peace be unto thee, brother Paphnutius," said Palemon; and he wiped the sweat from his forehead with his sleeve.

"Brother Palemon, all our discourse ought to be solely the praise of Him who has promised to be wheresoever two or three are gathered together in His Name. That is why I come to you concerning a design I have formed to glorify the Lord."

"May the Lord bless thy design, Paphnutius, as He has blessed my lettuces. Every morning He spreads His grace with the dew on my garden, and His goodness causes me to glorify Him in the cucumbers and melons which He gives me. Let us pray that He may keep us in His peace. For nothing is more to be feared than those unruly passions which trouble our hearts. When these passions disturb us we are like drunken men, and we stagger from right to left unceasingly, and are like to fall miserably. Sometimes these passions plunge us into a turbulent joy, and he who gives way to such, sullies the air with brutish laughter. Such false joy drags the sinner into all sorts of excess. But sometimes also the troubles of the soul and of the senses throw us into an impious sadness which is a thousand times worse than the joy. Brother Paphnutius, I am but a miserable sinner, but I have found, in my long life, that the cenobite has no foe worse than sadness. I mean by that the obstinate melancholy which envelopes the soul as in a mist, and hides from us the light of God. Nothing is more contrary to salvation, and the devil's greatest triumph is to sow black and bitter thoughts in the heart of a good man. If he sent us only pleasurable temptations, he would not be half so much to be feared. Alas! he excels in making us sad. Did he not show to our father Anthony a black child of such surpassing beauty that the very sight of it drew tears? With God's help, our father Anthony avoided the snares of the demon. I knew him when he lived amongst us; he was cheerful with his disciples, and never gave way to melancholy. But did you not come, my brother, to talk to me of a design you had formed in your mind? Let me know what it is — if, at least, this design has for its object the glory of God."

"Brother Palemon, what I propose is really to the glory of God. Strengthen me with your counsel, for you know many things, and sin has never darkened the clearness of your mind."

"Brother Paphnutius, I am not worthy to unloose the latchet of thy sandals, and my sins are as countless as the sands of the desert. But I am old, and I will never refuse the help of my experience."

"I will confide in you, then, brother Palemon, that I am stricken with grief at the thought that there is, in Alexandria, a courtesan named Thaïs, who lives in sin, and is a subject of reproach unto the people."

"Brother Paphnutius, that is, in truth, an abomination which we do well to deplore. There are many women amongst the Gentiles who lead lives of that kind. Have you thought of any remedy for this great evil?"

"Brother Palemon, I will go to Alexandria and find this woman, and, with God's help, I will convert her; that is my intention; do you approve of it, brother?"

"Brother Paphnutius, I am but a miserable sinner, but our father Anthony used to say, 'In whatsoever place thou art, hasten not to leave it to go elsewhere.'"

"Brother Palemon, do you disapprove of my project?"

"Dear Paphnutius, God forbid that I should suspect my brother of bad intentions. But our father Anthony also said, 'Fishes die on dry land, and so is it with those monks who leave their cells and mingle with the men of this world, amongst whom no good thing is to be found.'"

Having thus spoken, the old man pressed his foot on the spade, and began to dig energetically round a fig tree laden with fruit. As he was thus engaged, there was a rustling in the bushes, and an antelope leaped over the hedge which surrounded the garden; it stopped, surprised and frightened, its delicate legs trembling, then ran up to the old man, and laid its pretty head on the breast of its friend.

"God be praised in the gazelle of the desert," said Palemon.

He went to his hut, the light-footed little animal trotting after him, and brought out some black bread, which the antelope ate out of his hand.

Paphnutius remained thoughtful for some time, his eyes fixed upon the stones at his feet. Then he slowly walked back to his cell, pondering on what he had heard. A great struggle was going on in his mind.

"The hermit gives good advice," he said to himself; "the spirit of prudence is in him. And he doubts the wisdom of my intention. Yet it would be cruel to leave Thaïs any longer in the power of the demon who possesses her. May God advise and conduct me."

As he was walking along, he saw a plover, caught in the net that a hunter had laid on the sand, and he knew that it was a hen bird, for he saw the male fly to the net, and tear the meshes one by one with its beak, until it had made an opening by which its mate could escape. The holy man watched this incident, and as, by virtue of his holiness, he easily comprehended the mystic sense of all occurrences, he knew that the captive bird was no other than Thaïs, caught in the snares of sin, and that — like the plover that had cut the hempen threads with its beak — he could, by pronouncing the word of power, break the invisible bonds by which Thaïs was held in sin. Therefore he praised God, and was confirmed in his first resolution. But then seeing the plover caught by the feet, and hampered by the net it had broken, he fell into uncertainty again.

He did not sleep all night, and before dawn he had a vision. Thaïs appeared to him again. There was no expression of guilty pleasure on her face, nor was she dressed according to custom in transparent drapery. She was enveloped in a shroud, which hid even a part of her face, so that the Abbot could see nothing but the two eyes, from which flowed white and heavy tears.

At this sight he began to weep, and believing that this vision came from God, he no longer hesitated. He rose, seized a knotted stick, the symbol of the Christian faith, and left his cell, carefully closing the door, lest the animals of the desert and the birds of the air should enter, and befoul the copy of the Holy Scriptures which stood at the head of his bed. He called Flavian, the deacon, and gave him authority over the other twenty-three disciples during his absence; and then, clad only in a long cassock, he bent his steps towards the Nile, intending to follow the Libyan bank to the city founded by the Macedonian monarch. He walked from dawn to eve, indifferent to fatigue, hunger, and thirst; the sun was already low on the horizon when he saw the dreadful river, the blood-red waters of which rolled between the rocks of gold and fire.

He kept along the shore, begging his bread at the door of solitary huts for the love of God, and joyfully receiving insults, refusals, or threats. He feared neither robbers nor wild beasts, but he took great care to avoid all the towns and villages he came near. He was afraid lest he should see children playing at knuckle-bones before their father's house, or meet, by the side of the well, women in blue smocks, who might put down their pitcher and smile at him. All things are dangerous for the hermit; it is sometimes a danger for him to read in the Scriptures that the Divine Master journeyed from town to town and supped with His disciples. The virtues that the anchorites embroider so carefully on the tissue of faith, are as fragile as they are beautiful; a breath of ordinary life may tarnish their pleasant colors. For that reason, Paphnutius avoided the towns, fearing lest his heart should soften at the sight of his fellow men.

He journeyed along lonely roads. When evening came, the murmuring of the breeze amidst the tamarisk trees made him shiver, and he pulled his hood over his eyes that he might not see how beautiful all things were. After walking six days, he came to a place called Silsile. There the river runs in a narrow valley, bordered by a double chain of granite mountains. It was there that the Egyptians, in the days when they worshipped demons, carved their idols. Paphnutius saw an enormous sphinx carved in the solid rock. Fearing that it might still possess some diabolical properties, he made the sign of the cross, and pronounced the name of Jesus; he immediately saw a bat fly out of one of the monster's ears, and Paphnutius knew that he had driven out the evil spirits which had been for centuries in the figure. His zeal increased, and picking up a large stone, he threw it in the idol's face. Then the mysterious face of the sphinx expressed such profound sadness that Paphnutius was moved. In fact, the expression of superhuman grief on the stone visage would have touched even the most unfeeling man. Therefore Paphnutius said to the sphinx —

"O monster, be like the satyrs and centaurs our

father Anthony saw in the desert, and confess the divinity of Jesus Christ, and I will bless thee in the name of the Father, the Son, and the Holy Ghost."

When he had spoken a rosy light gleamed in the eyes of the sphinx; the heavy eyelids of the monster quiv-ered and the granite lips painfully murmured, as though in echo to the man's voice, the holy name of Jesus Christ; therefore Paphnutius stretched out his right hand, and blessed the sphinx of Silsile.

That being done, he resumed his journey, and the valley having grown wider, he saw the ruins of an immense city. The temples, which still remained stand-ing, were supported by idols which served as columns, and — by the permission of God — these figures with women's heads and cow's horns, threw on Paphnutius a long look which made him turn pale. He walked thus seventeen days, his only food a few raw herbs, and he slept at night in some ruined palace, amongst the wild cats and Pharaoh's rats, with which mingled some-times, women whose bodies ended in a scaly tail. But Paphnutius knew that these women came from hell, and he drove them away by making the sign of the cross.

On the eighteenth day, he found, far from any village, a wretched hut made of palm leaves, and half buried under the sand which had been driven by the desert wind. He approached it, hoping that the hut was inhabited by some pious anchorite. He saw inside the hovel — for there was no door — a pitcher, a bunch of onions, and a bed of dried leaves.

"This must be the habitation of a hermit," he said to himself. "Hermits are generally to be found near their hut, and I shall not fail to meet this one. I will give him the kiss of peace, even as the holy Anthony did when he came to the hermit Paul, and kissed him three times. We will discourse of things eternal, and perhaps our Lord will send us, by one of His ravens, a crust of bread, which my host will willingly invite me to share with him."

Whilst he was thus speaking to himself, he walked round the hut to see if he could find any one. He had not walked a hundred paces when he saw a man seated, with his legs crossed, by the side of the river. The man was naked; his hair and beard were quite white, and his body redder than brick. Paphnutius felt sure this must be the hermit. He saluted him with the words the monks are accustomed to use when they meet each other.

"Peace be with you, brother! May you some day taste the sweet joys of paradise."

The man did not reply. He remained motionless, and appeared not to have heard. Paphnutius supposed this was due to one of those rhapsodies to which the saints are accustomed. He knelt down, with his hands joined, by the side of the unknown, and remained thus in prayer till sunset. Then, seeing that his companion had not moved, he said to him —

"Father, if you are now out of the ecstasy in which you were lost, give me your blessing in our Lord Jesus Christ."

The other replied without turning his head —

"Stranger, I understand you not, and I know not the Lord Jesus Christ."

"What!" cried Paphnutius. "The prophets have announced Him; legions of martyrs have confessed His name; Cæsar himself has worshipped Him, and, but just now, I made the sphinx of Silsile proclaim His glory. Is it possible that you do not know Him?"

"Friend," replied the other, "it is possible. It would even be certain, if anything in this world were certain."

Paphnutius was surprised and saddened by the incredible ignorance of the man.

"If you know not Jesus Christ," he said, "all your works serve no purpose, and you will never rise to life immortal."

The old man replied —

"It is useless to act, or to abstain from acting. It matters not whether we live or die."

"Eh, what?" asked Paphnutius. "Do you not desire to live through all eternity? But, tell me, do you not live in a hut in the desert as the hermits do?"

"It seems so."

"Do I not see you naked, and lacking all things?"

"It seems so."

"Do you not feed on roots, and live in chastity?"

"It seems so."

"Have you not renounced all the vanities of this world?"

"I have truly renounced all those vain things for which men commonly care."

"Then you are like me, poor, chaste, and solitary. And you are not so — as I am — for the love of God, and with a hope of celestial happiness! That I cannot understand. Why are you virtuous if you do not believe in Jesus Christ? Why deprive yourself of the good things of this world if you do not hope to gain eternal riches in heaven?"

"Stranger, I deprive myself of nothing which is good, and I flatter myself that I have found a life which is satisfactory enough, though — to speak more precisely — there is no such thing as a good or evil life. Nothing is itself, either virtuous or shameful, just or unjust, pleasant or painful, good or bad. It is our opinion which gives those qualities to things, as salt gives savor to meats."

"So then, according to you there is no certainty. You deny the truth which the idolaters themselves have sought. You lie in ignorance — like a tired dog sleeping in the mud."

"Stranger, it is equally useless to abuse either dogs or philosophers. We know not what dogs are or what we are. We know nothing."

"Old man, do you belong, then, to the absurd sect of skeptics? Are you one of those miserable fools who alike deny movement and rest, and who know not how to distinguish between the light of the sun and the shadows of night?"

"Friend, I am truly a skeptic, and of a sect which appears praiseworthy to me, though it seems ridiculous to you. For the same things often assume different appearances. The pyramids of Memphis seem at sunrise to be cones of pink light. At sunset they look like black triangles against the illuminated sky. But who shall solve the problem of their true nature? You reproach me with denying appearances, when, in fact, appearances are the only realities I recognize. The sun seems to me illuminous, but its nature is unknown to me. I feel that fire burns — but I know not how or why. My friend, you understand me badly. Besides, it is indifferent to me whether I am understood one way or the other."

"Once more. Why do you live on dates and onions in the desert? Why do you endure great hardships? I endure hardships equally great, and, like you, I live in abstinence and solitude. But then it is to please God, and to earn eternal happiness. And that is a reasonable object, for it is wise to suffer now for a future gain. It is senseless, on the contrary, to expose yourself voluntarily to useless fatigue and vain sufferings. If I did not believe — pardon my blasphemy, O uncreated Light! — if I did not believe in the truth of that which God has taught us by the voice of the prophets, by the example of His Son, by the acts of the Apostles, by the authority of councils, and by the testimony of the martyrs, — if I did not know that the sufferings of the body are necessary for the salvation of the soul — if I were, like thee, lost in ignorance of sacred mysteries — I would return at once amongst the men of this day, I would strive to acquire riches, that I might live in ease, like those who are happy in this world, and I would say to the votaries of pleasure, 'Come, my daughters, come, my servants, come and pour out for me your wines, your philters, your perfumes.' But you, foolish old man! you deprive yourself of all these advantages; you lose without hope of any gain; you give without hope of any return, and you imitate foolishly the noble deeds of us anchorites, as an impudent monkey thinks, by smearing a wall, to copy the picture of a clever artist. What, then, are your reasons, O most besotted of men?"

Paphnutius spoke with violence and indignation, but the old man remained unmoved.

"Friend," he replied, gently, "what matter the reasons of a dog sleeping in the dirt or a mischievous ape?"

Paphnutius' only aim was the glory of God. His anger vanished, and he apologized with noble humility.

"Pardon me, old man, my brother," he said, "if zeal for the truth has carried me beyond proper bounds. God is my witness, that it is thy errors and not thyself that I hate. I suffer to see thee in darkness, for I love thee in Jesus Christ, and care for thy salvation fills my heart. Speak! give me your reasons. I long to know them that I may refute them."

The old man replied quietly —

"It is the same to me whether I speak or remain silent. I will give my reasons without asking yours in return, for I have no interest in you at all. I care neither for your happiness nor your misfortune, and it matters not to me whether you think one way or another. Why should I love you, or hate you? Aversion and sympathy are equally unworthy of the wise man. But since you question me, know then that I am named Timocles, and that I was born at Cos, of parents made rich by commerce. My father was a shipowner. In intelligence he much resembled Alexander, who is surnamed the Great. But he was not so gross. In short, he was a man of no great parts. I had two brothers, who, like him, were shipowners. As for me, I followed wisdom. My eldest brother was compelled by my father to marry a Carian woman, named Timaessa, who displeased him so greatly that he could not live with her without falling into a deep melancholy. However, Timaessa inspired our younger brother with a criminal passion, and this passion soon turned to a furious madness. The Carian woman hated them both equally; but she loved a flute-player, and received him at night in her chamber. One morning he left there the wreath which he usually wore at feasts. My two brothers, having found this wreath, swore to kill the flute player, and the next day they caused him to perish under the lash, in spite of his tears and prayers. My sister-in-law felt such grief that she lost her reason, and these three poor wretches became beasts rather than human beings, and wandered insane along the shores of Cos, howling like wolves and foaming at the mouth, and hooted at by the children, who threw shells and stones at them. They died, and my father buried them with his own hands. A little later his stomach refused all nourishment, and he died of hunger, though he was rich enough to have bought all the meats and fruits in the markets of Asia. He was deeply grieved at having to leave me his fortune. I used it in travels. I visited Italy, Greece, and Africa without meeting a single person who was either wise or happy. I studied philosophy at Athens and Alexandria, and was deafened by noisy arguments. At last I wandered as far as India, and I saw on the banks of the Ganges a naked man, who had sat there motionless with his legs crossed for more than thirty years. Climbing plants twined round his dried up body, and the birds built their nests in his hair. Yet he lived. At the sight of him I called to mind Timaessa, the flute-player, my two brothers, and my father, and I realized that this Indian was a wise man. 'Men,' I said to myself, 'suffer because they are deprived of that which they believe to be good; or because, possessing it they fear to lose it; or because they endure that which they believe to be an evil. Put an end to all beliefs of this kind, and the evils would disappear.' That is why I resolved henceforth to deem nothing an advantage, to tear myself entirely from the good things of this world, and to live silent and motionless, like the Indian."

Paphnutius had listened attentively to the old man's story.

"Timocles of Cos," he replied, "I own that your discourse is not wholly devoid of sense. It is, in truth, wise to despise the riches of this world. But it would be absurd to despise also your eternal welfare, and render yourself liable to be visited by the wrath of God. I grieve at your ignorance, Timocles, and I will instruct you in the truth, in order that knowing that there really exists a God in three hypostases, you may obey this God as a child obeys its father."

Timocles interrupted him.

"Refrain, stranger, from showing me your doctrines, and do not imagine that you will persuade me to share your opinions. All discussions are useless. My opinion is to have no opinion. My life is devoid of trouble because I have no preferences. Go thy ways, and strive not to withdraw me from the beneficent apathy in which I am plunged, as though in a delicious bath, after the hardships of my past days."

Paphnutius was profoundly instructed in all things relating to the faith. By his knowledge of the human heart, he was aware that the grace of God had not fallen on old Timocles, and the day of salvation for this soul so obstinately resolved to ruin itself had not yet come. He did not reply, lest the power given for edification should turn to destruction. For it sometimes happens, in disputing with infidels, that the means used for their conversion may steep them still farther in sin. Therefore they who possess the truth should take care how they spread it.

"Farewell, then, unhappy Timocles," he said; and heaving a deep sigh, he resumed his pious pilgrimage through the night.

In the morning, he saw the ibises motionless on one leg at the edge of the water, which reflected their pale pink necks. The willows stretched their soft grey foliage to the bank, cranes flew in a triangle in the clear sky, and the cry of unseen herons was heard from the sedges. Far as the eye could reach, the river rolled its broad green waters o'er which white sails, like the wings of birds, glided, and here and there on the shores, a white house shone out. A light mist floated along the banks, and from out the shadow of the islands, which were laden with palms, flowers, and fruits, came noisy flocks of ducks, geese, flamingoes, and teal. To the left, the grassy valley extended to the desert its fields and orchards in joyful abundance; the sun shone on the yellow wheat, and the earth exhaled forth its fecundity in odorous wafts. At this sight, Paphnutius fell on his knees, and cried —

"Blessed be the Lord, who has given a happy issue to my journey. O God, who spreadest Thy dew upon the fig trees of the Arsiniote, pour Thy grace upon Thaïs, whom Thou hast formed with Thy love, as Thou hast the flowers and trees of the field. May she, by Thy loving care, flourish like a sweet-scented rose in the heavenly Jerusalem."

And every time that he saw a tree covered with blossom, or a bird of brilliant plumage, he thought of Thaïs. Keeping along the left arm of the river and through a fertile and populous district, he reached, in a few days, the city of Alexandria, which the Greeks have surnamed the Beautiful and the Golden. The sun had risen an hour, when he beheld, from the top of a hill, the vast city, the roofs of which glittered in the rosy light. He stopped, and folded his arms on his breast.

"There, then," he said, "is the delightful spot where I was born in sin; the bright air where I breathed poisonous perfumes; the sea of pleasure where I heard the songs of the sirens. There is my cradle, after the flesh; my native land — in the parlance of the men of these days! A rich cradle, an illustrious country, in the judgment of men! It is natural that thy children should reverence thee like a mother, Alexandria, and I was begotten in thy magnificently adorned breast. But the ascetic despises nature, the mystic scorns appearances, the Christian regards his native land as a place of exile, the monk is not of this earth. I have turned away my heart from loving thee, Alexandria. I hate thee! I hate thee for thy riches, thy science, thy pleasures, and thy beauty. Be accursed, temple of demons! Lewd couch of the Gentiles, tainted pulpit of Arian heresy, be thou accursed! And thou, winged son of heaven who led the holy hermit Anthony, our father, when he came from the depths of the desert, and entered into the citadel of idolatry to strengthen the faith of believers and the confidence of martyrs, beautiful angel of the Lord, invisible child, first breath of God, fly thou before me, and cleanse, by the beating of thy wings, the corrupted air I am about to breathe amongst the princes of darkness of this world!"

Having thus spoken, he resumed his journey. He entered the city by the Gate of the Sun. This gate was a handsome structure of stone! In the shadow of its arch, crowded some poor wretches, who offered lemons and figs for sale, or with many groans and lamentations, begged for an obolus.

An old woman in rags, who was kneeling there, seized the monk's cassock, kissed it, and said —

"Man of the Lord, bless me, that God may bless me. I have suffered many things in this world that I may have joys in the world to come. You come from God, O holy man, and that is why the dust of your feet is more precious than gold."

"The Lord be praised!" said Paphnutius, and with his half-closed hand he made the sign of redemption on the old woman's head.

But hardly had he gone twenty paces down the street, than a band of children began to jeer at him, and throw stones, crying —

"Oh, the wicked monk! He is blacker than an ape, and more bearded than a goat! He is a skulker! Why not hang him in an orchard, like a wooden Priapus, to frighten the birds? But no; he would draw down the hail on the apple-blossom. He brings bad luck. To the ravens with the monk! to the ravens!" and stones mingled with the cries.

"My God, bless these poor children!" murmured Paphnutius.

And he pursued his way, thinking.

"I was worshipped by the old woman, and hated and despised by these children. Thus the same object is appreciated differently by men who are uncertain in their judgment and liable to error. It must be owned that, for a Gentile, old Timocles was not devoid of sense. Though blind, he knew he was deprived of light. His reasoning was much better than that of these idolaters, who cry from the depths of their thick darkness, 'I see the day!' Everything in this world is mirage and moving sand. God alone is steadfast."

He passed through the city with rapid steps. After ten years of absence he would still recognize every stone, and every stone was to him a stone of reproach that recalled a sin. For that reason he struck his naked feet roughly against the kerb-stones of the wide street, and rejoiced to see the bloody marks of his wounded feet. Leaving on his left the magnificent portico of the Temple of Serapis, he entered a road lined with splendid mansions, which seemed to be drowsy with perfumes. Pines, maples, and larches raised their heads above the red cornices and golden acroteria. Through the half-open doors could be seen bronze statues in marble vestibules, and fountains playing amidst foliage. No noise troubled the stillness of these quiet retreats. Only the distant strains of a flute could be heard. The monk stopped before a house, rather small, but of noble proportions, and supported by columns as graceful as young girls. It was ornamented with bronze busts of the most celebrated Greek philosophers.

He recognized Plato, Socrates, Aristotle, Epicurus, and Zeno, and having knocked with the hammer against the door, he waited, wrapped in meditation.

"It is vanity to glorify in metal these false sages; their lies are confounded, their souls are lost in hell, and even the famous Plato himself, who filled the earth with his eloquence, now disputes with the devils."

A slave opened the door, and seeing a man with bare feet standing on the mosaic threshold, said to him roughly —

"Go and beg elsewhere, stupid monk, or I will drive you away with a stick."

"Brother," replied the Abbott of Antinoë, "all that I ask is that you conduct me to your master, Nicias."

The slave replied, more angrily than before —

"My master does not see dogs like you."

"My son," said Paphnutius, "will you please do what I ask, and tell your master that I desire to see him.

"Get out, vile beggar!" cried the porter furiously; and he raised his stick and struck the holy man, who, with his arms crossed upon his breast, received unmovedly the blow, which fell full in his face, and then repeated gently —

"Do as I ask you, my son, I beg."

The porter tremblingly murmured —

"Who is this man who is not afraid of suffering?"

And he ran and told his master.

Nicias had just left the bath. Two pretty slave girls were scraping him with strigils. He was a pleasant-looking man, with a kind smile. There was an expression of gentle satire in his face. On seeing the monk, he rose and advanced with open arms.

"It is you!" he cried, "Paphnutius, my fellow scholar, my friend my brother! Oh, I knew you again, though, to say the truth, you look more like a wild animal than a man. Embrace me. Do you remember the time when we studied grammar, rhetoric, and philosophy together? You were, even then, of a morose and wild character, but I liked you because of your complete sincerity. We used to say that you looked at the universe with the eyes of a wild horse, and it was not surprising you were dull and moody. You needed a pinch of Attic salt, but your liberality knew no bounds. You cared nothing for either your money or your life. And you had the eccentricity of genius, and a strange character which interested me deeply. You are welcome, my dear Paphnutius, after ten years of absence. You have quitted the desert; you have renounced all Christian superstitions, and now return to your old life. I will mark this day with a white stone."

"Crobyle and Myrtale," he added, turning towards the girls, "perfume the feet, hands, and beard of my dear guest."

They smiled, and had already brought the basin, the phials, and the metal mirror. But Paphnutius stopped them with an imperious gesture, and lowered his eyes that he might not look upon them, for they were naked. Nicias brought cushions for him, and offered him various meats and drinks, which Paphnutius scornfully refused.

"Nicias," he said, "I have not renounced what you falsely call the Christian superstition, which is the truth of truths. 'In the beginning was the Word, and the Word was with God, and the Word was God. All things were made by Him, and without Him was not anything made that was made. In Him was the life, and the life was the light of men.'"

"My dear Paphnutius," replied Nicias, who had now put on a perfumed tunic, "do you expect to astonish me by reciting a lot of words jumbled together without skill, which are no more than a vain murmur? Have you forgotten that I am a bit of a philosopher myself? And do you think to satisfy me with some rags, torn by ignorant men from the purple garment of Æmilius, when Æmilius, Porphyry, and Plato, in all their glory, did not satisfy me! The systems devised by the sages are but tales imagined to amuse the eternal childishness of men. We divert ourselves with them, as we do with the stories of *The Ass, The Tub,* and *The Ephesian Matron,* or any other Milesian fable."

And, taking his guest by the arm, he led him into a room where thousands of papyri were rolled up and lay in baskets.

"This is my library," he said. "It contains a small part of the various systems which the philosophers have constructed to explain the world. The Serapeium itself, with all its riches, does not contain them all. Alas! they are but the dreams of sick men."

He compelled his guest to sit down in an ivory chair, and sat down himself. Paphnutius scowled gloomily at all the books in the library, and said —

"They ought all to be burned."

"Oh, my dear guest, that would be a pity!" replied Nicias. "For the dreams of sick men are sometimes amusing. Besides, if we should destroy all the dreams and visions of men, the earth would lose its form and colors, and we should all sleep in a dull stupidity."

Paphnutius continued in the same strain as before —

"It is certain that the doctrines of the pagans are but vain lies. But God, who is the truth, revealed Himself to men by miracles, and He was made flesh, and lived among us."

Nicias replied —

"You speak well, my dear Paphnutius, when you say that he was made flesh. A God who thinks, acts, speaks, who wanders through nature, like Ulysses of old on the glaucous sea, is altogether a man. How do you expect that we should believe in this new Jupiter, when the urchins of Athens, in the time of Pericles, no longer believed in the old one?

"But let us leave all that. You did not come here; I suppose, to argue about the three hypostases. What can I do for you, my dear fellow scholar?"

"A good deed," replied the Abbot of Antinoë. "Lend me a perfumed tunic, like the one you have just put on. Be kind enough to add to the tunic, gilt sandals, and a vial of oil to anoint my beard and hair. It is needful also, that you should give me a purse with a thousand drachmæ in it. That, O Nicias, is what I came to ask of you, for the love of God, and in remembrance of our old friendship.":

Nicias made Crobyle and Myrtale bring his richest tunic; it was embroidered, after the Asiatic fashion, with flowers and animals. The two girls held it open, and skillfully showed its bright colors, waiting till Paphnutius should have taken off the cassock which covered him down to his feet. But the monk having declared that they should rather tear off his flesh than this garment, they put on the tunic over it. As the two girls were pretty, they were not afraid of men, although they were slaves. They laughed at the strange appearance of the monk thus clad. Crobyle called him her dear satrap, as she presented him with the mirror, and Myrtale pulled his beard. But Paphnutius prayed to the Lord, and did not look at them. Having tied on the gilt sandals, and fastened the purse to his belt, he said to Nicias, who was looking at him with an amused expression —

"O Nicias, let not these things be an offence in your eyes. For know that I shall make pious use of this tunic, this purse, and these sandals."

"My dear friend," replied Nicias, "I suspect no evil, for I believe that men are equally incapable of doing evil or doing good. Good and evil exist only in the opinion. The wise man has only custom and usage to guide him in his acts. I conform with all the prejudices which prevail at Alexandria. That is why I pass for an honest man. Go, friend, and enjoy yourself."

But Paphnutius thought that it was needful to inform his host of his intention.

"Do you know Thaïs," he said, "who acts in the games at the theatre?"

"She is beautiful," replied Nicias, "and there was a time when she was dear to me. For her sake, I sold a mill and two fields of corn, and I composed in her honor three books full of detestably bad verses. Surely beauty is the most powerful force in the world, and were we so made that we could possess it always, we should care as little as may be for the demiurgos, the logos, the æons, and all the other reveries of the philosophers. But I am surprised, my good Paphnutius, that you should have come from the depths of the Thebaid to talk about Thaïs."

Having said this, he sighed gently. And Paphnutius gazed at him with horror, not conceiving it possible that a man should so calmly avow such a sin. He expected to see the earth open, and Nicias swallowed up in flames. But the earth remained solid, and the Alexandrian silent, his forehead resting on his hand, and he smiling sadly at the memories of his past youth. The monk rose, and continued in solemn tones —

"Know then, O Nicias, that, with the aid of God, I will snatch this woman Thaïs from the unclean affections of the world, and give her as a spouse to Jesus Christ. If the Holy Spirit does not forsake me, Thaïs will leave this city and enter a nunnery."

"Beware of offending Venus," replied Nicias. "She is a powerful goddess, she will be angry with you if you take away her chief minister."

"God will protect me," said Paphnutius. "May He also illumine thy heart, O Nicias, and draw thee out of the abyss in which thou art plunged."

And he stalked out of the room. But Nicias followed him, and overtook him on the threshold, and placing his hand on his shoulder whispered into his ear the same words —

"Beware of offending Venus; her vengeance is terrible."

Paphnutius, disdainful of these trivial words, left without turning his head. He felt only contempt for Nicias; but what he could not bear was the idea that his former friend had received the caresses of Thaïs. It seemed to him that to sin with that woman was more detestable than to sin with any other. To him this appeared the height of iniquity, and he henceforth looked upon Nicias as an object of execration. He had always hated impurity, but never before had this vice appeared so heinous to him; never before had it so seemed to merit the anger of Jesus Christ and the sorrow of the angels.

He felt only a more ardent desire to save Thaïs from the Gentiles, and that he must hasten to see the actress in order to save her. Nevertheless, before he could enter her house, he must wait till the heat of the day was over, and now the morning had hardly finished. Paphnutius wandered through the most frequented streets. He had resolved to take no food that day, in order to be the less unworthy of the favors he had asked of the

Lord. To the great grief of his soul, he dared not enter any of the churches in the city, because he knew they were profaned by the Arians, who had overturned the Lord's table. For, in fact, these heretics, supported by the Emperor of the East, had driven the patriarch Athanasius from his episcopate, and sown trouble and confusion among the Christians of Alexandria.

He therefore wandered about aimlessly, sometimes with his eyes fixed on the ground in humility, and sometimes raised to heaven in ecstasy. After some time, he found himself on the quay. Before him lay the harbor, in which were sheltered innumerable ships and galleys, and beyond them, smiling in blue and silver, lay the perfidious sea. A galley, which bore a Nereid at its prow, had just weighed anchor. The rowers sang as the oars struck the water; and already the white daughter of the waters, covered with humid pearls, showed no more than a flying profile to the monk. Steered by her pilot, she cleared the passage leading from the basin of the Eunostos, and gained the high seas, leaving a glittering trail behind her.

"I also," thought Paphnutius, "once desired to embark singing on the ocean of the world. But I soon saw my folly, and the Nereid did not carry me away."

Lost in his thoughts, he sat down upon a coil of rope, and went to sleep. During his sleep, he had a vision. He seemed to hear the sound of a clanging trumpet, and the sky became blood red, and he knew that the day of judgment had come. Whilst he was fervently praying to God, he saw an enormous monster coming towards him, bearing on its forehead a cross of light, and he recognized the sphinx of Silsile. The monster seized him between its teeth, without hurting him, and carried him in its mouth, as a cat carries a kitten. Paphnutius was thus conveyed across many countries, crossing rivers and traversing mountains, and came at last to a desert place, covered with scowling rocks and hot cinders. The ground was rent in many places, and through these openings came a hot air. The monster gently put Paphnutius down on the ground, and said —

"Look!"

And Paphnutius, leaning over the edge of the abyss, saw a river of fire which flowed in the interior of the earth, between two cliffs of black rocks. There, in a livid light, the demons tormented the souls of the damned. The souls preserved the appearance of the bodies which had held them, and even wore some rags of clothing. These souls seemed peaceful in the midst of their torments. One of them, tall and white, his eyes closed, a white fillet across his forehead, and a scepter in his hand, sang; his voice filled the desert shores with harmony; he sang of gods and heroes. Little green devils pierced his lips and throat with red-hot irons. And the shade of Homer still sang. Near by, old Anaxagoras, bald and hoary, traced figures in the dust with a compass. A demon poured boiling oil into his ear, yet failed, however, to disturb the sage's meditations. And the monk saw many other persons, who, on the dark shore by the side of the burning river, read, or quietly meditated, or conversed with other spirits while walking, — like the sages and pupils under the shadow of the sycamore trees of Academe. Old Timocles alone had withdrawn from the others, and shook his head like a man who denies. One of the demons of the abyss shook a torch before his eyes, but Timocles would see neither the demon nor the torch.

Mute with surprise at this spectacle, Paphnutius turned to the monster. It had disappeared, and, in place of the sphinx, the monk saw a veiled woman, who said —

"Look and understand. Such is the obstinacy of these infidels, that, even in hell, they remain victims of the illusions which deluded them when on earth. Death has not undeceived them; for it is very plain that it does not suffice merely to die in order to see God. Those who are ignorant of the truth whilst living, will be ignorant of it always. The demons which are busy torturing these souls, what are they but agents of divine justice? That is why these souls neither see them nor feel them. They were ignorant of the truth, and therefore unaware of their own condemnation, and God Himself cannot compel them to suffer.

"God can do all things," said the Abbot of Antinoë.

"He cannot do that which is absurd," replied the veiled woman. "To punish them, they must first be enlightened, and if they possessed the truth, they would be like unto the elect."

Vexed and horrified, Paphnutius again bent over the edge of the abyss. He saw the shade of Nicias smiling, with a wreath of flowers on his head, sitting under a burnt myrtle tree. By his side was Aspasia of Miletus, gracefully draped in a woolen cloak, and they seemed to talk together of love and philosophy; the expression of her face was sweet and noble. The rain of fire which fell on them was as a refreshing dew, and their feet pressed the burning soil as though it had been tender grass. At this sight Paphnutius was filled with fury.

"Strike him, O God! strike him!" he cried. "It is Nicias! Let him weep! let him groan! let him grind his teeth! He sinned with Thaïs!"

And Paphnutius woke in the arms of a sailor, as strong as Hercules, who cried —

"Quietly! quietly! my friend! By Proteus, the old shepherd of the seals, you slumber uneasily. If I had not caught hold of you, you would have tumbled into the Eunostos. It is as true as that my mother sold salt fish, that I saved your life."

"I thank God," replied Paphnutius.

And, rising to his feet, he walked straight before him, meditating on the vision which had come to him whilst he was asleep.

"This vision," he said to himself, "is plainly an evil one; it is an insult to divine goodness to imagine hell is unreal. The dream certainly came from the devil."

He reasoned thus because he knew how to distinguish between the dreams sent by God and those produced by evil angels. Such discernment is useful to the hermit, who lives surrounded by apparitions, and who, in avoiding men, is sure to meet with spirits. The deserts are full of phantoms. When the pilgrims drew near the ruined castle, to which the holy hermit, Anthony, had retired, they heard a noise like that which goes up from the public square of a large city at a great festival. The noise was made by the devils, who were tempting the holy man.

Paphnutius remembered this memorable example. He also called to mind St. John the Egyptian, who for sixty years was tempted by the devil. But John saw through all the tricks of the demon. One day, however, the devil, having assumed the appearance of a man, entered the grotto of the venerable John, and said to him, "John, you must continue to fast until tomorrow evening." And John, believing that it was an angel who spoke, obeyed the voice of the demon, and fasted the next day until the vesper hour. That was the only victory that the Prince of Darkness ever gained over St. John the Egyptian, and that was but a trifling one. It was therefore not astonishing that Paphnutius knew at once that the vision which had visited him in his sleep was an evil one.

Whilst he was gently remonstrating with God for having given him into the power of the demons, he felt himself pushed and dragged amidst a crowd of people who were all hurrying in the same direction. As he was unaccustomed to walk in the streets of a city, he was shoved and knocked from one passer to another like an inert mass; and being embarrassed by the folds

of his tunic, he was more than once on the point of
falling. Desirous of knowing where all these people
could be going, he asked one of them the cause of this
hurry.

"Do you not know, stranger," replied he, "that the
games are about to begin, and that Thaïs will appear
on the stage? All the citizens are going to the theatre,
and I also am going. Would you like to accompany
me?"

It occurred to him at once that it would further his
design to see Thaïs in the games, and Paphnutius
followed the stranger. In front of them stood the
theatre, its portico ornamented with shining masks,
and its huge circular wall covered with innumerable
statues. Following the crowd, they entered a narrow
passage, at the end of which lay the amphitheatre,
glittering with light. They took their places on one of
the seats, which descended in steps to the stage, which
was empty but magnificently decorated. There was no
curtain to hide the view, and on the stage was a mound,
such as used to be erected in old times to the shades
of heroes. This mound stood in the midst of a camp.
Lances were stacked in front of the tents, and golden
shields hung from masts, amidst boughs of laurel and
wreaths of oak. On the stage all was silence, but a
murmur like the humming of bees in a hive rose from
the vast hemicycle filled with spectators. All their faces,
reddened by the reflection from the purple awning
which waved above them, turned with attentive curiosity towards the large, silent stage, with its tomb and
tents. The women laughed and ate lemons, and the
regular theatre-goers called gaily to one another from
their seats.

Paphnutius prayed inwardly, and refrained from
uttering any vain words, but his neighbor began to
complain of the decline of the drama.

"Formerly," he said, "clever actors used to declaim,

under a mask, the verses of Euripides and Menander. Now they no longer recite dramas, they act in dumb show; and of the divine spectacles with which Bacchus was honored in Athens, we have kept nothing but what a barbarian — a Scythian even — could understand — attitude and gesture. The tragic mask, the mouth of which was provided with metal tongues that increased the sound of the voice; the cothurnus, which raised the actors to the height of gods; the tragic majesty and the splendid verses that used to be sung, have all gone. Pantomimists, and dancing girls with bare faces, have replaced Paulus and Roscius. What would the Athenians of the days of Pericles have said if they had seen a woman on the stage? It is indecent for a woman to appear in public. We must be very degenerate to permit it. It is as certain as that my name is Dorion, that woman is the natural enemy of man, and a disgrace to human kind."

"You speak wisely," replied Paphnutius; "woman is our worst enemy. She gives us pleasure, and is to be feared on that account."

"By the immovable gods," cried Dorion, "it is not pleasure that woman gives to man, but sadness, trouble, and black cares. Love is the cause of our most biting evils. Listen, stranger. When I was a young man I visited Troezene, in Argolis, and I saw there a myrtle of a most prodigious size, the leaves of which were covered with innumerable pinholes. And this is what the Troezenians say about that myrtle. Queen Phædra, when she was in love with Hippolytos, used to recline idly all day long under this same tree. To beguile the tedium of her weary life she used to draw out the golden pin which held her fair locks, and pierce with it the leaves of the sweet-scented bush. All the leaves were riddled with holes. After she had ruined the poor young man whom she pursued with her incestuous love, Phædra, as you know, perished miserably. She locked herself up in her bridal chamber, and hanged herself by her golden girdle from an ivory peg. The gods willed that the myrtle, the witness of her bitter misery, should continue to bear, in its fresh leaves, the marks of the pin-holes. I picked one of these leaves, and placed it at the head of my bed, that by the sight of it I might take warning against the folly of love, and conform to the doctrine of the divine Epicurus, my master, who taught that all lust is to be feared. But, properly speaking, love is a disease of the liver, and one is never sure of not catching the malady."

Paphnutius asked —

"Dorion, what are your pleasures?"

Dorion replied sadly —

"I have only one pleasure, and, it must be confessed, that it is not a very exciting one; it is meditation. When a man has a bad digestion, he must not look for any others."

Taking advantage of these words, Paphnutius proceeded to initiate the Epicurean into those spiritual joys which the contemplation of God procures. He began —

"Hear the truth, Dorion, and receive the light."

But he saw then that all heads were turned towards him, and everybody was making signs for him to be quiet. Dead silence prevailed in the theatre, broken at last by the strains of heroic music.

The play began. The soldiers left their tents, and were preparing to depart, when a prodigy occurred — a cloud covered the summit of the funeral pile. Then the cloud rolled away, and the ghost of Achilles appeared, clad in golden armor. Extending his arms towards the warriors, he seemed to say to them, "What! do you depart, children of Danaos? do you return to the land I shall never behold again, and leave my tomb without any offerings?" Already the principal Greek chieftains pressed to the foot of the pile. Acamas, the son of

Theseus, old Nestor, Agamemnon, bearing a scepter and with a fillet on his brow, gazed at the prodigy. Pyrrhus, the young son of Achilles, was prostrate in the dust. Ulysses, recognizable by the cap which covered his curly hair, showed by his gestures that he acquiesced in the demand of the hero's shade. He argued with Agamemnon, and their words might be easily guessed —

"Achilles," said the King of Ithaca, "is worthy to be honored by us, for he died gloriously for Hellas. He demands that the daughter of Priam, the virgin Polyxena, should be immolated on his tomb. Greeks! appease the manes of the hero, and let the son of Peleus rejoice in Hades."

But the king of kings replied —

"Spare the Trojan virgins we have torn from the altars. Sufficient misfortunes have already fallen on the illustrious race of Priam."

He spoke thus because he shared the couch of the sister of Polyxena, and the wise Ulysses reproached him for preferring the couch of Cassandra to the lance of Achilles.

The Greeks showed they shared the opinion of Ulysses, by loudly clashing their weapons. The death of Polyxena was resolved on, and the appeased shade of Achilles vanished. The music — sometimes wild and sometimes plaintive — followed the thoughts of the personages in the drama. The spectators burst into applause.

Paphnutius, who applied divine truth to everything murmured —

"This fable shows how cruel the worshippers of false gods were."

"All religions breed crimes," replied the Epicurean. "Happily, a Greek, who was divinely wise, has freed men from foolish terrors of the unknown —"

Just at that moment, Hecuba, her white hair disheveled, her robe tattered, came out of the tent in which she was kept captive. A long sigh went up from the audience, when her woeful figure appeared. Hecuba had been warned by a prophetic dream, and lamented her daughter's fate and her own. Ulysses approached her, and asked her to give up Polyxena. The old mother tore her hair, dug her nails into her cheeks, and kissed the hands of the cruel chieftain, who, with unpitying calmness, seemed to say —

"Be wise, Hecuba, and yield to necessity. There are amongst us many old mothers who weep for their children, now sleeping under the pines of Ida."

And Hecuba, formerly queen of the most flourishing city in Asia, and now a slave, bowed her unhappy head in the dust.

Then the curtain in front of one of the tents was raised, and the virgin Polyxena appeared. A tremor passed through all the spectators. They had recognized Thaïs. Paphnutius saw again the woman he had come to seek. With her white arm she held above her head the heavy curtain. Motionless as a splendid statue, she stood, with a look of pride and resignation in her violet eyes, and her resplendent beauty made a shudder of commiseration pass through all who beheld her.

A murmur of applause uprose, and Paphnutius, his soul agitated, and pressing both hands to his heart, sighed —

"Why, O my God, hast thou given this power to one of Thy creatures?"

Dorion was not so disturbed. He said —

"Certainly the atoms, which have momentarily met together to form this woman, present a combination which is agreeable to the eye. But that is but a freak of nature, and the atoms know not what they do. They will some day separate with the same indifference as they came together. Where are now the atoms which formed Lais or Cleopatra? I must confess that women

are sometimes beautiful. But they are liable to grievous
afflictions, and disgusting inconveniences. That is pat-
ent to all thinking men, though the vulgar pay no
attention to it. And women inspire love, though it is
absurd and ridiculous to love them."

Such were the thoughts of the philosopher and the
ascetic as they gazed on Thaïs. They neither of them
noticed Hecuba, who turned to her daughter, and
seemed to say by her gestures —

"Try to soften the cruel Ulysses. Employ your tears,
your beauty, and your youth."

Thaïs — or rather Polyxena herself — let fall the
curtain of the tent. She made a step forward, and all
hearts were conquered. And when, with firm but light
steps, she advanced towards Ulysses, her rhythmic
movements, which were accompanied by the sound of
flutes, created in all present such happy visions, that it
seemed as though she were the divine center of all the
harmonies of the world. All eyes were bent on her; the
other actors were obscured by her effulgence, and were
not noticed. The play continued, however.

The prudent son of Laertes turned away his head,
and hid his hand under his mantle, in order to avoid
the looks and kisses of the suppliant. The virgin made
a sign to him to fear nothing. Her tranquil gaze said —

"I follow you, Ulysses, and bow to necessity — because I wish to die. Daughter of Priam, and sister of
Hector, my couch, which was once worthy of Kings,
shall never receive a foreign master. Freely do I quit the
light of day."

Hecuba, lying motionless in the dust, suddenly rose
and enfolded her daughter in a last despairing embrace. Polyxena gently, but resolutely, removed the old
arms which held her. She seemed to say —

"Do not expose yourself, mother, to the fury of your
master. Do not wait until he drags you ignominiously
on the ground in tearing me from your arms. Better,

O well-beloved mother, to give me your wrinkled hand, and bend your hollow cheeks to my lips."

The face of Thaïs looked beautiful in its grief. The crowd felt grateful to her for showing them the forms and passions of life endowed with superhuman grace, and Paphnutius pardoned her present splendor on account of her coming humility, and glorified himself in advance for the saint he was about to give to heaven.

The drama neared its end. Hecuba fell as though dead, and Polyxena, led by Ulysses, advanced towards the tomb, which was surrounded by the chief warriors. A dirge was sung as she mounted the funeral pile, on the summit of which the son of Achilles poured out libations from a gold cup to the manes of the hero. When the sacrificing priests stretched out their arms to seize her, she made a sign that she wished to die free and unbound, as befitted the daughter of so many kings. Then, tearing aside her robe, she bared her bosom to the blow. Pyrrhus, turning away his head, plunged his sword into her heart, and by a skilful trick, the blood gushed forth over the dazzling white breast of the virgin, who, with head thrown back, and her eyes swimming in the horrors of death, fell with grace and modesty.

Whilst the warriors enshrouded the victim with a veil, and covered her with lilies and anemones, terrified screams and groans rent the air, and Paphnutius, rising from his seat, prophesied in a loud voice.

"Gentiles? vile worshippers of demons! And you Arians more infamous than the idolaters! — learn! That which you have just seen is an image and a symbol. There is a mystic meaning in this fable, and very soon the woman you see there will be offered, a willing and happy sacrifice, to the risen God."

But already the crowd was surging in dark waves towards the exits. The Abbot of Antinoë, escaping from the astonished Dorion, gained the door, still prophesying.

An hour later he knocked at the door of the house of Thaïs.

The actress then lived in the rich Racotis quarter, near the tomb of Alexander, in a house surrounded by shady gardens, in which a brook, bordered with poplars, flowed amidst artificial rocks. An old black slave woman, loaded with rings, opened the door, and asked what he wanted.

"I wish to see Thaïs," he replied. "God is my witness that I came here for no other purpose."

As he wore a rich tunic, and spoke in an imperious manner, the slave allowed him to enter.

"You will find Thaïs," she said, "in the Grotto of Nymphs."

PART THE SECOND

The Papyrus

*T*haïs was born of free, but poor, parents, who were idolaters. When she was a very little girl, her father kept, at Alexandria, near the Gate of the Moon, an inn, which was frequented by sailors. She still retained some vivid, but disconnected, memories of her early youth. She remembered her father, seated at the corner of the hearth with his legs crossed — tall, formidable, and quiet, like one of those old Pharaohs who are celebrated in the ballads sung by blind men at the street corners. She remembered also her thin, wretched mother, wandering like a hungry cat about the house, which she filled with the tones of her sharp voice, and the glitter of her phosphorescent eyes. They said in the neighborhood that she was a witch, and changed into an owl at night, and flew to see her lovers. It was a lie. Thaïs knew well, having often watched her, that her mother practiced no magic arts, but that she was eaten up with avarice, and counted all night the gains of the day. The idle father and the greedy mother let the child live as best it could, like one of the fowls in the poultry-yard. She became very clever in extracting, one by one, the oboli from the belt of some drunken sailor, and in amusing the drinkers with artless songs and obscene words, the meaning of which she did not know. She passed from knee to knee, in a room reeking with the odors of fermented drinks and resiny wineskins; then, her cheeks sticky with beer and pricked by rough beards, she escaped, clutching the oboli in her little hand, and ran to buy honey-cakes from an old woman who crouched behind her baskets under the Gate of the Moon. Every day the same scenes were repeated, the sailors relating their perilous adventures, then playing at dice or knuckle-bones, and blaspheming the gods, amid their shouting for the best beer of Cilicia.

Every night the child was awakened by the quarrels of the drunkards. Oyster-shells would fly across the tables, cutting the heads of those they hit, and the uproar was terrible. Sometimes she saw, by the light of the smoky lamps, the knives glitter, and the blood flow.

It humiliated her to think that the only person who showed her any human kindness in her young days was the mild and gentle Ahmes. Ahmes, the house-slave, a Nubian blacker than the pot he gravely skimmed, was as good as a long night's sleep. Often he would take Thaïs on his knee, and tell her old tales about underground treasure-houses constructed for avaricious kings, who put to death the masons and architects. There were also tales about clever thieves who married kings' daughters, and courtesans who built pyramids. Little Thaïs loved Ahmes like a father, like a mother, like a nurse, and like a dog. She followed the slave into the cellar when he went to fill the amphorae, and into the poultry-yard amongst the scraggy and ragged fowls, all beak, claws, and feathers, who flew swifter than eagles before the knife of the black cook. Often at night, on the straw, instead of sleeping, he built for Thaïs little water-mills, and ships no bigger than his hand, with all their rigging.

He had been badly treated by his masters; one of his ears was torn, and his body covered with scars. Yet his features always wore an air of joyous peace. And no one ever asked him whence he drew the consolation in his soul, and the peace in his heart. He was as simple as a child. As he performed his heavy tasks, he sang, in a harsh voice, hymns which made the child tremble and dream. He murmured, in a gravely joyous tone —

"Tell us, Mary, what thou hast seen where thou hast
        been?
I saw the shroud and the linen cloths, and the an-
        gels seated on the tomb.
And I saw the glory of the Risen One."

She asked him —
"Father, why do you sing about angels seated on a tomb?"
And he replied —
"Little light of my eyes, I sing of the angels because Jesus, our Lord, is risen to heaven."

Ahmes was a Christian. He had been baptised, and was known as Theodore at the meetings of the faithful, to which he went secretly during the hours allowed him for sleep.

At that time the Church was suffering the severest trials. By order of the Emperor, the churches had been thrown down, the holy books burned, the sacred vessels and candlesticks melted. The Christians had been deprived of all their honors, and expected nothing but death. Terror reigned over all the community at Alexandria, and the prisons were crammed with victims. It was whispered with horror amongst the faithful, that in Syria, in Arabia, in Mesopotamia, in Cappadocia, in all the empire, bishops and virgins had been flogged, tortured, crucified or thrown to wild beasts. Then Anthony, already celebrated for his visions and his solitary life, a prophet, and the head of all the Egyptian believers, descended like an eagle from his desert rock on the city of Alexandria, and, flying from church to church, fired the whole community with his holy ardor. Invisible to the pagans, he was present at the same time at all the meetings of Christians, endowing all with the spirit of strength and prudence by which he was animated. Slaves, in particular, were persecuted with singular severity. Many of them, seized with fright, denied the faith. Others, and by far the greater number, fled to the desert, hoping to live there, either as hermits or robbers. Ahmes, however, frequented the meetings as usual, visited the prisoners, buried the martyrs, and joyfully professed the religion of Christ. The great Anthony, who saw his unshaken zeal, before he returned into the desert, pressed the black slave in his arms, and gave him the kiss of peace.

When Thaïs was seven years old, Ahmes began to talk to her of God.

"The good Lord God," he said, "lived in heaven like a Pharaoh, under the tents of His harem, and under the trees of His gardens. He was the Ancient of Ancients, and older than the world; and He had but one Son, the Prince Jesus, whom He loved with all His heart, and who surpassed in beauty the virgins and the angels. And the good Lord God said to Prince Jesus —

" 'Leave My harem and My palace, and My date trees and My running waters. Descend to earth for the welfare of men. There Thou shalt be like a little child, and Thou shalt live poor amongst the poor. Suffering shall be Thy daily bread, and Thou shalt weep so profusely that Thy tears shall form rivers, in which the tired slave shall bathe with delight. Go, My Son!'

"Prince Jesus obeyed the good Lord, and He came down to earth, to a place named Bethlehem of Judea. And He walked in fields, amidst the flowering anemones, saying to His companion —

" 'Blessed are they who hunger, for I will lead them to My Father's table! Blessed are they who thirst, for they shall drink of the fountains of heaven! Blessed are they who weep, for I will dry their tears with veils finer than those of the almehs!'

"That is why the poor loved Him, and believed in Him. But the rich hated Him; fearing that He should raise the poor above them. At that time, Cleopatra and Cæsar were powerful on the earth. They both hated Jesus, and they ordered the judges and priests to put Him to death. To obey the Queen of Egypt, the princes of Syria erected a cross on a high mountain, and they caused Jesus to die on this cross. But women washed His corpse, and buried it; and Prince Jesus, having broken the door of His tomb, rose again to the good Lord, His Father.

"And, from that time, all those who believed in Him go to heaven.

"The Lord God opens His arms, and says to them —

" 'Ye are welcome, because ye love the Prince, My Son. Wash, and then eat.'

"They bathe to the sound of beautiful music, and, all the time they are eating, they see almehs dancing, and they listen to tales that never end. They are dearer to the good Lord God than the light of His eyes, because they are His guests, and they shall have for their portion the carpets of His house, and the pomegranates of His gardens."

Ahmes often spoke in this strain, and thus taught the truth to Thaïs. She wondered, and said —

"I should like to eat the pomegranates of the good Lord."

Ahmes replied —

"Only those who are baptised may taste the fruits of heaven."

And Thaïs asked to be baptised. Seeing by this that she believed in Jesus, the slave resolved to instruct her more fully, so that, being baptised, she might enter the Church; and he loved her as his spiritual daughter.

The child, unloved and uncared for by its selfish parents, had no bed in the house. She slept in a corner of the stable amongst the domestic animals, and there Ahmes came to her every night secretly.

He gently approached the mat on which she lay, and sat down on his heels, his legs bent and his body straight — a position hereditary to his race. His face and his body, which was clothed in black, were invisible in the darkness; but his big white eyes shone out, and there came from them a light like a ray of dawn through the chinks of a door. He spoke in a husky, monotonous tone, with a slight nasal twang that gave it the soft melody of music heard at night in the streets. Sometimes the breathing of an ass, or the soft lowing of an ox, accompanied, like a chorus of invisible spirits, the voice of the slave as he recited the gospels. His words flowed gently in the darkness, which they filled with zeal, mercy, and hope; and the neophyte, her hand in that of Ahmes, lulled by the monotonous sounds, and the vague visions in her mind, slept calm and smiling, amid the harmonies of the dark night and the holy mysteries, gazed down on by a star, which twinkled between the joists of the stable-roof.

The initiation lasted a whole year, till the time when the Christians joyfully celebrate the festival of Easter. One night in the holy week, Thaïs, who was already asleep on her mat, felt herself lifted by the slave, whose eyes gleamed with a strange light. He was clad, not as usual in a pair of torn drawers, but in a long white cloak, beneath which he pressed the child, whispering to her —

"Come, my soul! Come, light of my eyes! Come, little sweetheart! Come and be clad in the baptismal robes!"

He carried the child pressed to his breast. Frightened

and yet curious, Thaïs, her head out of the cloak, threw her arms round her friend's neck, and he ran with her through the darkness. They went down narrow, black alleys; they passed through the Jews' quarter; they skirted a cemetery, where the osprey uttered its dismal cry; they traversed an open space, passing under crosses on which hung the bodies of victims, and on the arms of the crosses the ravens clacked their beaks. Thaïs hid her head in the slave's breast. She did not dare to peep out all the rest of the way. Soon it seemed to her that she was going down under ground. When she reopened her eyes she found herself in a narrow cave, lighted by resin torches, on the walls of which were painted standing figures, which seemed to move and live in the flickering glare of the torches. They were men clad in long tunics and carrying branches of palm, and around them were lambs, doves, and tendrils of vine.

Amongst these figures, Thaïs recognized Jesus of Nazareth, by the anemones flowering at his feet. In the center of the cave, near a large stone font filled with water, stood an old man clad in a scarlet dalmatic embroidered with gold, and on his head a low miter. His thin face ended in a long beard. He looked gentle and humble, in spite of his rich costume. This was Bishop Vivantius, an exiled dignitary of the Church of Cyrene, who now gained his livelihood by weaving common stuffs of goats' hair. Two poor children stood by his side. Close by, an old Negress unfolded a little white robe. Ahmes set the child down on the ground, and kneeling before the Bishop, said —

"Father, this is the little soul, the child of my soul. I have brought her that you may, according to your promise, and if it please your holiness, bestow on her the baptism of life."

At these words the Bishop opened his arms, and showed his mutilated hands. His nails had been torn out because he had maintained the faith in the days of persecution. Thaïs was frightened, and threw herself into the arms of Ahmes. But the kind words of the priest reassured her.

"Fear nothing, dearly beloved little one. Thou hast here a spiritual father, Ahmes, who is called Theodore amongst the faithful, and a kind mother in grace, who has prepared for thee, with her own hands, a white robe."

And turning towards the Negress —

"She is called Nitida," he added, "and is a slave in this world, but in heaven she will be a spouse of Jesus."

Then he said to the child neophyte —

"Thaïs, dost thou believe in God, the Father Almighty; and in His only Son, who died for our salvation; and in all that the apostles taught?"

"Yes," replied together the Negro and Negress, who held her by each hand.

By the Bishop's orders, Nitida knelt down and undressed Thaïs. The child was quite naked; round her neck was an amulet. The Pontiff plunged her three times into the baptismal font. The acolytes brought the oil, with which Vivantius anointed the catechumen, and the salt, a morsel of which he placed on her tongue. Then, having dried that body which was destined, after many trials, to life immortal, the slave Nitida put on Thaïs the white robe she had woven.

The Bishop gave to each and all the kiss of peace, and, the ceremony being terminated, took off his sacerdotal insignia.

When they had left the crypt, Ahmes said —

"We ought to rejoice that we have this day brought a soul to the good Lord God; let us go to the house of your Holiness and spend the rest of the night in rejoicing."

"Thou hast well said, Theodore," replied the Bishop, and he led the little band to his house, which was quite near. It consisted of a single room, furnished with a couple of looms, a heavy table, and a worn-out carpet. As soon as they had entered,

"Nitida," cried the Nubian, "bring hither the stove and the jar of oil, and we will have a good supper."

Saying thus, he drew from under his cloak some little fish which he had kept concealed, and lighted a fire and fried them. The Bishop, the girl, the two boys, and the two slaves sat in a ring on the carpet, ate the fried fish, and blessed the Lord. Vivantius spoke of the torture he had undergone, and prophesied the speedy triumph of the Church. His language was grotesque, and full of word-play and rhetorical tropes. He compared the life of the just to a tissue of purple, and to explain the mystery of baptism, he said —

"The Divine Spirit floated on the waters, and that is why Christians receive the baptism of water. But demons also inhabit the brooks; springs consecrated to nymphs are especially dangerous, and there are certain waters which cause various maladies, both of the soul and of the body."

Sometimes he spoke enigmatically, and the child listened to him with profound awe and wonder. At the end of the repast he offered his guests a little wine, and this unloosed their tongues, and they began to sing lamentations and hymns. Ahmes and Nitida then rose, and danced a Nubian dance which they had learned as children, and which, no doubt, had been danced by their tribe since the early ages of the world. It was a love dance; waving their arms, and moving their bodies in rhythmic measure, they feigned, in turn, to fly from and to pursue each other. Their big eyes rolled, and they showed their gleaming teeth in broad grins.

In this strange manner did Thaïs receive the holy rite of baptism.

She loved amusements, and, as she grew, vague desires were created in her mind. All day long she danced and sang with the children in the streets, and when at

night she returned to her father's house, she was still
singing —

"Crooked twist, why do you stay in the house?
I comb the wool, and the Miletan threads.
Crooked twist, what did your son die of?
He fell from the white horses into the sea."

She now began to prefer the company of boys and
girls to that of the gentle and quiet Ahmes. She did
not notice that her friend was not so often with her.
The persecution having relented, the Christians were
able to assemble more regularly, and the Nubian frequented these meetings assiduously. His zeal increased,
and he sometimes uttered mysterious threats. He said
that the rich would not keep their wealth. He went to
the public places to which the poorer Christians used
to resort, and assembling together all the poor wretches
who were lying in the shade of the old walls, he announced to them that all slaves would soon be free,
and that the day of justice was at hand.

"In the kingdom of God," he said, "the slaves will
drink new wine and eat delicious fruits; whilst the rich,
crouching at their feet like dogs, will devour the
crumbs from their table."

These sayings were noised abroad through all that
quarter of the city, and the masters feared that Ahmes
might incite the slaves to revolt. The innkeeper hated
him intensely, though he carefully concealed his ran-
cor.

One day, a silver salt-cellar, reserved for the table of
the gods, disappeared from the inn. Ahmes was accused
of having stolen it — out of hate to his master and to
the gods of the empire. There was no proof of the
accusation, and the slave vehemently denied the
charge. Nevertheless, he was dragged before the tribunal, and as he had the reputation of being a bad servant,

the judge condemned him to death.

"As you did not know how to make a good use of your hands," he said, "they will be nailed to the cross."

Ahmes heard the verdict quietly, bowed to the judge most respectfully, and was taken to the public prison. During the three days that remained to him, he did not cease to preach the gospel to the prisoners, and it was related afterwards that the criminals, and the gaoler himself, touched by his words, believed in Jesus crucified.

He was taken to the very place which one night, less than two years before, he had crossed so joyfully, carrying in his cloak little Thaïs, the daughter of his soul, his darling flower. When his hands were nailed to the cross, he uttered no complaint, but many times he sighed and murmured, "I thirst."

His agony lasted three days and three nights. It seemed hardly possible that human flesh could have endured such prolonged torture. Many times it was thought he was dead; the flies clustered on his eyelids, but suddenly he would reopen his bloodshot eyes. On the morning of the fourth day, he sang, in a voice clearer and purer than that of a child —

"Tell us, Mary, what thou hast seen where thou hast been?"

Then he smiled and said —

"They come, the angels of the good Lord. They bring me wine and fruit. How refreshing is the fanning of their wings!"

And he expired.

His features preserved in death an expression of ecstatic happiness. Even the soldiers who guarded the cross were struck with wonder. Vivantius, accompanied by some of the Christian brethren, claimed the body, and buried it with the remains of the other martyrs in the crypt of St. John the Baptist, and the Church venerated the memory of Saint Theodore the Nubian.

Three years later, Constantine, the conqueror of Maxentius, issued an edict which granted toleration to the Christians, and the believers were not henceforth persecuted, except by heretics.

Thaïs had completed her eleventh year when her friend was tortured to death, and she felt deeply saddened and shocked. Her soul was not sufficiently pure to allow her to understand that the slave Ahmes was blessed both in his life and his death. The idea sprang up in her little mind that no one can be good in this world except at the cost of the most terrible sufferings. And she was afraid to be good, for her delicate flesh could not bear pain.

At an early age, she had given herself to the lads about the port, and she followed the old men who wandered about the quarter in the evening, and with what she received from them she bought cakes and trinkets.

As she did not take home any of the money she gained, her mother continually ill-treated her. To get out of reach of her mother's arm, she often ran, barefooted, to the city walls, and hid with the lizards. There she thought with envy of the ladies she had seen pass her, richly dressed, and in a litter surrounded by slaves.

One day, when she had been beaten more brutally than usual, she was crouching down beside the gate, motionless and sulky, when an old woman stopped in front of her, looked at her for some moments in silence, and then cried —

"Oh, the pretty flower! the beautiful child! Happy is the father who begot thee, and the mother who brought thee into the world!"

Thaïs remained silent, with her eyes fixed on the ground. Her eyelids were red, and it was evident she had been weeping.

"My white violet," continued the old woman, "is not your mother happy to have nourished a little goddess like you, and does not your father, when he sees you, rejoice from the bottom of his heart?"

To which the child replied, as though talking to herself —

"My father is a wine-skin swollen with wine, and my mother a greedy horse-leech."

The old woman glanced to right and left, to see if she were observed. Then, in a fawning voice —

"Sweet flowering hyacinth, beautiful drinker of light, come with me, and you shall have nothing to do but dance and smile. I will feed you on honey cakes, and my son — my own son — will love you as his eyes. My son is handsome and young; he has but little beard on his chin; his skin is soft, and he is, as they say, a little Acharnian pig."

Thaïs replied —

"I am quite willing to go with you."

And she rose and followed the old woman out of the city.

The old woman, who was named Moeroë, went from city to city with a troupe of girls and boys, whom she taught to dance, and then hired out to rich people to appear at feasts.

Guessing that Thaïs would soon develop into a most beautiful woman, she taught her — with the help of a whip — music and prosody, and she flogged with leather thongs those beautiful legs, when they did not move in time to the strains of the cithara. Her son — a decrepit abortion, of no age and no sex — ill-treated the child, on whom he vented the hate he had for all womankind. Like the dancing-girls whose grace he affected, he knew, and taught Thaïs, the art of panto-mime, and how to mimic, by expression, gesture, and attitude, all human passions, and more especially the passions of love. He was a clever master, though he disliked his work; but he was jealous of his pupil, and as soon as he discovered that she was born to give men pleasure, he scratched her cheeks, pinched her arms, or pricked her legs, as a spiteful girl would have done. Thanks, however, to his lessons, she quickly became an excellent musician, pantomimist, and dancer. The brutality of her master did not at all surprise her; it seemed natural to her to be badly treated. She even felt some respect for the old woman, who knew music and drank Greek wine. Moeroë, when she came to Antioch, praised her pupil to the rich merchants of the city who gave banquets, both as a dancer and a flute-player. Thaïs danced and pleased. She accompanied the rich bankers, when they left the table, into the shady groves on the banks of the Orontes. She gave herself to all, for she knew nothing of the price of love. But one night that she had danced before the most fashionable young men of the city, the son of the pro-consul came to her, radiant with youth and pleasure, and said, in a voice that seemed redolent of kisses —

"Why am I not, Thaïs, the wreath which crowns your hair, the tunic which enfolds your beautiful form, the sandal on your pretty foot? I wish you to tread me under foot as a sandal; I wish my caresses to be your tunic and your wreath. Come, sweet girl! come to my house, and let us forget the world."

She looked at him whilst he was speaking, and saw that he was handsome. Suddenly she felt a cold sweat on her face. She turned green as grass; she reeled; a cloud descended before her eyes. He again implored her to come with him, but she refused. His ardent looks, his burning words were vain, and when he took her in his arms to try and drag her away, she pushed him off rudely. Then he implored her, and shed tears. But a new, unknown, and invincible passion dominated her heart, and she still resisted.

"What madness!" said the guests. "Lollius is noble, handsome, and rich, and a dancing-girl treats him with scorn!"

Lollius returned home alone that night, quite love-sick. He came in the morning, pale and red-eyed, and hung flowers at the dancing-girl's door.

But Thaïs was frightened and troubled; she avoided Lollius, and yet he was continually in her mind. She suffered, and she did not know the cause of her complaint. She wondered why she had thus changed, and why she was melancholy. She recoiled from all her lovers; they were hateful to her. She loathed the light of day, and lay on her bed all day, sobbing, and with her head buried in the pillows. Lollius contrived to gain admittance, and came many times, but neither his pleadings nor his execrations had any effect on the obdurate girl. In his presence, she was as timid as a virgin, and would say nothing but —

"I will not! I will not!"

But at the end of a fortnight she gave in, for she knew that she loved him; she went to his house and lived with him. They were supremely happy. They passed their days shut up together, gazing into each other's eyes, and babbling a childish jargon. In the evening, they walked on the lonely banks of the Orontes, and lost themselves in the laurel woods. Sometimes they rose at dawn, to go and gather hyacinths on the slopes of Sulpicus. They drank from the same cup, and he would take a grape from between her lips with his mouth.

Moeroë came to Lollius, and cried and shrieked that Thaïs should be restored to her.

"She is my daughter," she said, "my daughter, who has been torn from me. My perfumed flower — my own bowels — !"

Lollius gave her a large sum of money, and sent her away. But, as she came back to demand some more gold staters, the young man had her put in prison, and the magistrates having discovered that she was guilty of many crimes, she was condemned to death, and thrown to the wild beasts.

Thaïs loved Lollius with all the passion of her mind, and the bewilderment of innocence. She told him, and told him truly from the bottom of her heart —

"I have never loved any one but you."

Lollius replied —

"You are not like any other woman."

The spell lasted six months, but it broke at last. Thaïs suddenly felt that her heart was empty and lonely. Lollius no longer seemed the same to her. She thought —

"What can have thus changed me in an instant? How is it that he is now like any other man, and no longer like himself?"

She left him, not without a secret desire to find Lollius again in another, as she no longer found him in himself. She thought it would be less dull to live with someone she had never loved, than with one she had ceased to love. She appeared, in the company of rich debauchees, at those sacred feasts at which naked virgins danced in the temples, and troops of courtesans swam across the Orontes. She took part in all the pleasures of the fashionable and depraved city; and she assiduously frequented the theatres, at which clever mimes from all countries performed amidst the applause of a crowd greedy for excitement.

She carefully observed the mimes, dancers, comedians, and especially the women, who in tragedies represented goddesses in love with young men, or mortals loved by the gods. Having discovered the secrets by which they pleased the audience, she thought to herself that she was more beautiful and could act better. She went to the manager, and asked to be admitted into the troupe. Thanks to her beauty, and to the lessons she had received from old Moeroë, she was received, and appeared on the stage in the part of Dircé.

She met with but indifferent success, for she was inexperienced, and the admiration of the spectators had not been aroused by hearing her praises sung. But after she had played small parts for a few months, the power of her beauty burst forth with such effect that all the city was moved. All Antioch crowded to the theatre. The imperial magistrates and the chief citizens were compelled, by the force of public opinion, to show themselves there. The porters, sweepers, and dock laborers went without bread and garlic, that they might pay for their places. Poets composed epigrams in her honor. Bearded philosophers inveighed against her in the baths and gymnasia; when her litter passed, Christian priests turned away their heads. The threshold of her door was wreathed with flowers, and sprinkled with blood. She received so much money from her lovers that it was no longer counted, but measured by the medimnus, and all the treasure hoarded by miserly old men was poured out at her feet. But she was placid and unmoved. She rejoiced, with quiet pride, in the admiration of the public and the favor of the gods, and was so much loved that she loved herself.

After she had several years enjoyed the admiration and affection of the Antiochians, she was taken with a desire to revisit Alexandria, and show her glory in that city in which, as a child, she had wandered in want and shame, hungry and lean as a grasshopper in the middle of a dusty road. The golden city joyfully welcomed her, and loaded her with fresh riches; when she appeared in the games it was a triumph. Countless admirers and lovers came to her. She received them with indifference, for she at last despaired of meeting another Lollius.

Amongst many others, she met the philosopher Nicias, who desired to possess her, although he professed to have no desires. In spite of his riches, he was intelligent and modest. But his delicate wit and beautiful sentiments failed to charm her. She did not love him and sometimes his refined irony even irritated her. His perpetual doubts hurt her, for he believed in nothing, and she believed in everything. She believed in divine providence, in the omnipotence of evil spirits, in spells, exorcisms, and eternal justice; she believed in Jesus Christ, and in the goddess of good of the Syrians; she believed also that bitches barked when black Hecate passed through the streets, and that a woman could inspire love by pouring a philter into a cup wrapped in the bleeding skin of a sheep. She thirsted for the unknown; she called on nameless gods, and lived in perpetual expectation. The future frightened her, and yet she wished to know it. She surrounded herself with priests of Isis, Chaldean magi, pharmacopolists, and professors of the black arts, who invariably deceived her, though she never tired of being deceived. She feared death, and she saw it everywhere. When she yielded to pleasure, it seemed to her that an icy finger would suddenly touch her on the bare shoulder, and she turned pale, and cried with terror, in the arms which embraced her.

Nicias said to her —

"What does it matter, O my Thaïs, whether we descend to eternal night with white locks and hollow cheeks, or, whether this very day, now laughing to the vast sky, shall be our last? Let us enjoy life; we shall have greatly lived if we have greatly loved. There is no knowledge except that of the senses; to love is to understand. That which we do not know does not exist. What good is it to worry ourselves about nothing?"

She replied angrily —

"I despise men like you, who hope for nothing and fear nothing. I wish to *know!* I wish to *know!*"

In order to understand the secret of life, she set to work to read the books of the philosophers, but she did not understand them. The further the years of her childhood receded from her, the more anxious she was to recall them. She loved to traverse at night, in disguise, the alleys, squares, and places where she had grown up so miserably. She was sorry she had lost her parents, and especially that she had not been able to love them. When she met any Christian priest, she thought of her baptism, and felt troubled. One night, when enveloped in a long cloak, and her fair hair hidden under a black hood, she was wandering, according to custom, about the suburbs of the city, she found herself — without knowing how she came there — before the poor little church of St. John the Baptist. They were singing inside the church, and a bright light glimmered through the chinks of the door. There was nothing strange in that, as, for the past twenty years, the Christians, protected by the conqueror of Maxentius, had publicly solemnized their festivals. But these hymns seemed more like an ardent appeal to the soul. As if she had been invited to the mysteries, she pushed the door open with her arm, and entered the building. She found a numerous assembly of women, children, and old men, on their knees before a tomb, which stood against the wall. The tomb was nothing but a stone coffer, roughly sculptured with vine tendrils and bunches of grapes; yet it had received great honors, and was covered with green palms and wreaths of red roses. All round, innumerable lights gleamed out of the heavy shadow, in which the smoke of Arabian gums seemed like the folds of angels' robes, and the paintings on the walls visions of Paradise. Priests, clad in white, were prostrate at the foot of the sarcophagus. The hymns they sang with the people expressed the delight of suffering, and mingled, in a triumphal mourning, so much joy with so much grief, that Thaïs, in listening to them, felt the pleasures of life and the terrors of death flowing, at the same time, through her re-awakened senses.

When they had finished singing, the believers rose, and walked in single file to the tomb, the side of which they kissed. They were common men, accustomed to work with their hands. They advanced with a heavy step, the eyes fixed, the jaw dropped, but they had an air of sincerity. They knelt down, each in turn, before the sarcophagus, and put their lips to it. The women lifted their little children in their arms, and gently placed their cheek to the stone.

Thaïs, surprised and troubled, asked a deacon why they did so.

"Do you not know, woman," replied the deacon, "that we celebrate today the blessed memory of St. Theodore the Nubian, who suffered for the faith in the days of the Emperor Diocletian? He lived virtuously and died a martyr, and that is why, robed in white, we bear red roses to his glorious tomb."

On hearing these words, Thaïs fell on her knees, and burst into tears. Half-forgotten recollections of Ahmes returned to her mind. On the memory of this obscure, gentle, and unfortunate man, the blaze of candles, the perfume of roses, the clouds of incense, the music of hymns, the piety of souls, threw all the charms of glory. Thaïs thought in the dazzling glare —

"He was good, and now he has become great and glorious. Why is it that he is elevated above other men? What is this unknown thing which is more than riches or pleasure?"

She rose slowly, and turned towards the tomb of the saint who had loved her, those violet eyes, now filled with tears which glittered in the candle-light; then, with bowed head, humble, slow, and the last, with those lips on which so many desires hung, she kissed the stone of the slave's tomb.

When she returned to her house, she found Nicias, who, with his hair perfumed, and his tunic thrown open, was reading a treatise on morals whilst waiting for her. He advanced with open arms.

"Naughty Thaïs," he said, in a laughing voice, "whilst I was waiting for you to come, do you know what I saw in this manuscript, written by the gravest of Stoics? Precepts of virtue and noble maxims: No! On the staid papyrus, I saw dance thousands and thousands of little Thaïses. Each was no bigger than my finger, and yet their grace was infinite, and all were the only Thaïs. There were some who flaunted in mantles of purple and gold; others, like a white cloud, floated in the air in transparent drapery. Others again, motionless and divinely nude, the better to inspire pleasure, expressed no thought. Lastly, there were two, hand in hand; two so alike that it was impossible to distinguish one from the other. Both smiled. The first said, 'I am love.' The other, 'I am death.'"

Thus speaking, he pressed Thaïs in his arms, and not noticing the sullen look in her downcast eyes, he went on adding thought to thought, heedless of the fact that they were all lost upon her.

"Yes, when I had before my eyes the line in which it was written, 'Nothing should deter you from improving your mind,' I read, 'The kisses of Thaïs are warmer than fire, and sweeter than honey.' That is how a philosopher reads the books of other philosophers — and that is your fault, you naughty child. It is true that, as long as we are what we are, we shall never find anything but our own thoughts in the thoughts of others, and that all of us are somewhat inclined to read books as I have read this one."

She did not hear him; her soul was still before the Nubian's tomb. As he heard her sigh, he kissed her on the neck, and said —

"Do not be sad, my child. We are never happy in this world, except when we forget the world.

"Come, let us cheat life — it is sure to take its revenge. Come, let us love!"

But she pushed him away.

"*We* love!" she cried bitterly. "*You* never loved any one. And *I* do not love *you!* No! I do not love you! I hate you! Go! I hate you! I curse and despise all who are happy, and all who are rich! Go! Go! Goodness is only found amongst the unfortunate. When I was a child I knew a black slave who died on the cross. He was good; he was filled with love, and he knew the secret of life. You are not worthy to wash his feet. Go! I never wish to see you again!"

She threw herself on her face on the carpet, and passed the night sobbing and weeping, and forming resolutions to live, in future, like Saint Theodore, in poverty and humbleness.

The next day, she devoted herself again to those pleasures to which she was addicted. As she knew that her beauty, though still intact, would not last very long, she hastened to derive all the enjoyment and all the fame she could from it. At the theatre, where she acted and studied more than ever, she gave life to the imagination of sculptors, painters, and poets. Recognizing that there was in the attitudes, movements, and walk of the actress, an idea of the divine harmony which rules the spheres, wise men and philosophers considered that such perfect grace was a virtue in itself, and said, "Thaïs also is a geometrician!" The ignorant, the poor, the humble, and the timid before whom she consented to appear, regarded her as a blessing from heaven. Yet she was sad amidst all the praise she received, and dreaded death more than ever. Nothing was able to set her mind at rest, not even her house and gardens, which were celebrated, and a proverb throughout the city.

The gardens were planted with trees, brought at great expense from India and Persia. They were watered by a running brook, and colonnades in ruins, and imitation rocks, arranged by a skilful artist, were reflected in a lake, which also mirrored the statues that stood round it. In the middle of the garden was the Grotto of Nymphs, which owed its name to three life-size figures of women, which stood on the threshold. They were represented as divesting themselves of their garments, and about to bathe. They anxiously turned their heads, fearing to be seen, and looked as though they were alive. The only light which entered the building came, tempered and iridescent, through thin sheets of water. All the walls were hung — as in the sacred grottoes — with wreaths, garlands, and votive pictures, in which the beauty of Thaïs was celebrated. There were also tragic and comic masks, bright with colors; and paintings representing theatrical scenes or grotesque figures, or fabulous animals. On a stele in the center stood a little ivory Eros of wonderful antique workmanship. It was a gift from Nicias. In one of the bays was a figure of a goat in black marble, with shining agate eyes. Six alabaster kids crowded round its teats; but, raising its cloven hoofs and its ugly head, it seemed impatient to climb the rocks. The floor was covered with Byzantine carpets, pillows embroidered by the yellow men of Cathay, and the skins of Libyan lions. Perfumed smoke arose from golden censers. Flowering plants grew in large onyx vases. And at the far end, in the purple shadow, gleamed the gold nails on the shell of a huge Indian tortoise turned upside down, which served as the bed of the actress. It was here that every day, to the murmur of the water, and amid perfumes and flowers, Thaïs reclined softly, and conversed with her friends, while awaiting the hour of supper, or meditated in solitude on theatrical art, or on the flight of years.

On the afternoon after the games, Thaïs was reposing in the Grotto of Nymphs. She had noticed in her mirror the first signs of the decay of her beauty, and she was frightened to think that white hair and wrinkles would at last come. She vainly tried to comfort herself with the assurance that she could recover her fresh complexion by burning certain herbs and pronouncing a few magic words. A pitiless voice cried, "You will grow old Thaïs; you will grow old." And a cold sweat of terror bedewed her forehead. Then, on looking at herself again in the mirror with infinite tenderness, she found that she was still beautiful and worthy to be loved. She smiled to herself, and murmured, "There is not a woman in Alexandria who can rival me in suppleness or grace or movement, or in splendor of arms, and the arms, my mirror, are the real chains of love!"

While she was thus thinking she saw an unknown man — thin, with burning eyes and unkempt beard, and clad in a richly embroidered robe — standing before her. She let fall her mirror, and uttered a cry of fright.

Paphnutius stood motionless, and seeing how beautiful she was, he murmured this prayer from the bottom of his heart —

"Grant, my God, that the face of this woman may not be a temptation, but may prove salutary to Thy servant."

Then, forcing himself to speak, he said —

"Thaïs, I live in a far country, and the fame of thy beauty has led me to thee. It is said that thou art the most clever of actresses and the most irresistible of women. That which is related of thy riches and thy love affairs seems fabulous, and calls to mind the old story of Rhodope, whose marvelous history is known by heart to all the boatmen on the Nile. Therefore I was seized with a desire to know thee, and I see that the truth surpasses the rumor. Thou art a thousand times more clever and more beautiful than is reported. And now that I see thee, I say to myself, 'It is impossible to approach her without staggering like a drunken man.'"

The words were feigned; but the monk, animated by pious zeal, uttered them with real warmth. Thaïs gazed, without displeasure, at this strange being who had frightened her. The rough, wild aspect, and the fiery glances of his eyes, astonished her. She was curious to learn the state of life of a man so different from all others she had met. She replied, with gentle raillery —

"You seem prompt to admire, stranger. Beware that my looks do not consume you to the bones! Beware of loving me!"

He said —

"I love thee, O Thaïs! I love thee more than my life, and more than myself. For thee I have quitted the desert; for thee my lips — vowed to silence — have pronounced profane words; for thee I have seen what I ought not to have seen, and heard what it was forbidden to me to hear; for thee my soul is troubled, my heart is open, and the thoughts gush out like the running springs at which the pigeons drink; for thee I have walked day and night across sandy deserts teeming with reptiles and vampires; for thee I have placed my bare foot on vipers and scorpions! Yes, I love thee! I love thee, but not like those men who, burning with the lusts of the flesh, come to thee like devouring wolves or furious bulls. Thou art dear to them as is the gazelle to the lion. Their ravening lusts will consume thee to the soul, O woman! I love thee in spirit and in truth; I love thee in God, and for ever and ever; that which is in my breast is named true zeal and divine charity. I promise thee better things than drunkenness crowned with flowers or the dreams of a brief night. I promise thee holy feasts and celestial suppers. The happiness that I bring thee will never end; it is un-heard-of, it is ineffable, and such that if the happy of this world could only see a shadow of it they would die of wonder."

Thaïs laughed mischievously.

"Friend," she said, "show me this wonderful love. Make haste! Long speeches would be an insult to my beauty; let us not lose a moment. I am impatient to taste the felicity you announce; but, to say the truth, I fear that I shall always remain ignorant of it, and that all you have promised me will vanish in words. It is easier to promise a great happiness than to give it. Everyone has a talent of some sort. I fancy that yours is to make long speeches. You speak of an unknown love. It is so long since kisses were first exchanged that it would be very extraordinary if there still remained secrets in love. On this subject lovers know more than philosophers."

"Do not jest, Thaïs. I bring thee the unknown love."

"Friend, you come too late. I know every kind of love."

"The love that I bring thee abounds with glory, whilst the loves that thou knowest breed only shame."

Thaïs looked at him with an angry eye, a frown gathered on her beautiful face.

"You are very bold, stranger, to offend your hostess. Look at me, and say if I resemble a creature crushed down with shame. No, I am not ashamed, and all others who live like me are not ashamed either, although they are not so beautiful or so rich as I am. I have sown pleasure in my footsteps, and I am celebrated for that all over the world. I am more powerful than the masters of the world. I have seen them at my feet. Look at me, look at these little feet; thousands of men would pay with their blood for the happiness of kissing them. I am not very big, and I do not occupy much space on the earth. To those who look at me from the top of the Serapeium, when I pass in the street, I look like a grain of rice; but that grain of rice has caused among men, griefs, despairs, hates, and crimes enough to have filled Tartarus. Are you not mad to talk to me of shame when all around proclaims my glory?"

"That which is glory in the eyes of men, is infamy before God. O woman, we have been nourished in countries so different, that it is not surprising we have neither the same language nor the same thoughts! Yet Heaven is my witness that I wish to agree with thee, and that it is my intention not to leave thee until we share the same sentiments. Who will inspire me with burning words that will melt thee like wax in my breath, O woman, that the fingers of my desires may mould thee as they wish? What virtue will deliver thee to me, O dearest of souls, that the spirit which animates me, creating thee a second time, may imprint on thee a fresh beauty, and that thou mayest cry, weeping for joy, 'It is only now that I am born'? Who will cause to gush in my heart a fount of Siloam, in which thou mayest bathe and recover thy first purity? Who will change me into a Jordan, the waves of which sprinkled on thee, will give thee life eternal?"

Thaïs was no longer angry.

"This man," she thought, "talks of life eternal and all that he says seems written on a talisman. No doubt he is a mage, and knows secret charms against old age and death," and she resolved to offer herself to him. Therefore, pretending to be afraid of him, she retired a few steps to the end of the grotto, and sitting down on the edge of the bed, artfully pulled her tunic across her breast; then, motionless and mute and her eyes cast down, she waited. Her long eyelashes made a soft shadow on her cheeks. Her entire attitude expressed modesty; her naked feet swung gently, and she looked like a child sitting thinking on the bank of a brook. But Paphnutius looked at her, and did not move. His trembling knees hardly supported him, his tongue dried in his mouth, a terrible buzzing rang in his ears. But all at once his sight failed, and he could see nothing before him but a thick cloud. He thought that the hand of Jesus had been laid on his eyes, to hide this woman from them. Reassured by such succor, strengthened and fortified, he said with a gravity worthy of an old hermit of the desert —

"If thou givest thyself to me, thinkest thou it is hidden from God?"

She shook her head.

"God? Who forces Him to keep His eye always upon the Grotto of Nymphs? Let Him go away if we offend Him! But why should we offend Him? Since He has created us, He can be neither angry nor surprised to see us as He made us, and acting according to the nature He has given us. A good deal too much is said on His behalf, and He is often credited with ideas He never had. You yourself, stranger, do you know His true character? Who are you that you should speak to me in His name?"

At this question the monk, opening his borrowed robe, showed the cassock, and said —

"I am Paphnutius, Abbot of Antinoë, and I come from the holy desert. The hand that drew Abraham from Chaldaea and Lot from Sodom has separated me from the present age. I no longer existed for the men of this century. But thy image appeared to me in my sandy Jerusalem, and I knew that thou wert full of corruption, and death was in thee. And now I am before thee, woman, as before a grave, and I cry unto thee, 'Thaïs, arise!'"

At the words, Paphnutius, monk, and abbot, she had turned pale with fright. And now, with disheveled hair and joined hands, weeping and groaning, she dragged herself to the feet of the saint.

"Do not hurt me! Why have you come? What do you want of me? Do not hurt me! I know that the saints of the desert hate women who, like me, are made to please. I am afraid that you hate me, and want to hurt me. Go! I do not doubt your power. But know, Paphnutius, that you should neither despise me nor hate me. I have never, like many of the men I know, laughed at your voluntary poverty. In your turn, do not make a crime of my riches. I am beautiful, and clever in acting. I no more chose my condition than my nature. I was made for that which I do. I was born to charm men. And you yourself, did you not say just now that you loved me? Do not use your science against me. Do not pronounce magic words which would destroy my beauty, or change me into a statue of salt. Do not terrify me! I am already too frightened. Do not kill me! I am so afraid of death."

He made a sign to her to rise, and said —

"Child, have no fear. I will utter no word of shame or scorn. I come on behalf of Him who sat on the edge of the well, and drank of the pitcher which the woman of Samaria offered to Him; and who, also, when He supped at the house of Simon, received the perfumes of Mary. I am not without sin that I should throw the first stone. I have often badly employed the abundant grace which God has bestowed upon me. It was not anger, but pity, which took me by the hand to conduct me here. I can, without deceit, address thee in words of love, for it is the zeal in my heart which has brought me to thee. I burn with the fire of charity, and if thy eyes, accustomed only to the gross sights of the flesh, could see things in their mystic aspect, I should appear unto thee as a branch broken off the burning bush which the Lord showed on the mountain to Moses of old, that he might understand true love — that which envelops us, and which, so far from leaving behind it mere coals and ashes, purifies and perfumes for ever that which it penetrates."

"I believe you, monk, and no longer fear either deceit or ill-will from you. I have often heard talk of the hermits of the Thebaid. Marvelous things have been told concerning Anthony and Paul. Your name is not unknown to me, and I have heard say that, though you are still young, you equal in virtue the oldest anchorites. As soon as I saw you, and without knowing who you were, I felt that you were no ordinary man. Tell me! can you do for me that which neither the priests of Isis, nor of Hermes, nor of the celestial Juno, nor the Chaldean soothsayers, nor the Babylonian magi have been able to effect? Monk, if you love me, can you prevent me from dying?"

"Woman, whosoever wishes to live shall live. Flee from the abominable delights in which thou diest for ever. Snatch from the devils, who will burn it most horribly, that body which God kneaded with His spittle and animated with his own breath. Thou art consumed with weariness; come, and refresh thyself at the blessed springs of solitude; come and drink of those fountains which are hidden in the desert, and which gush forth to heaven. Careworn soul, come, and possess that which thou desirest! Heart greedy for joy, come and taste true joys — poverty, retirement, self-forgetfulness, seclusion in the bosom of God. Enemy of Christ now, and tomorrow His well-beloved, come to Him! Come, thou whom I have sought, and thou wilt say, 'I have found love!'"

Thaïs seemed lost in meditation on things afar.

"Monk," she asked, "if I adjure all pleasures and do penance, is it true that I shall be born again in heaven, my body intact in all its beauty?"

"Thaïs, I bring thee eternal life. Believe me, for that which I announce to thee is the truth."

"Who will assure me that it is the truth?"

"David and the prophets, the Scriptures, and the wonders that thou shalt behold."

"Monk, I should like to believe you, for I must confess that I have not found happiness in this world. My lot in life is better than that of a queen, and yet I have many bitternesses and misfortunes, and I am infinitely weary of my existence. All women envy me, and yet sometimes I have envied the lot of a toothless old woman who, when I was a child, sold honey-cakes under one of the city gates. Often has the idea flashed across my mind that only the poor are good, happy, and blessed, and that there must be great gladness in living humble and obscure. Monk, you have agitated a storm in my soul, and brought to the surface that which lay at the bottom. Who am I to believe, alas! and what is to become of me — and what is life?"

Whilst she thus spoke, Paphnutius was transfigured; celestial joy beamed in his face.

"Listen!" he said. "I was not alone when I entered this house. Another accompanied me, another who stands by my side. Him thou canst not see, because thy eyes are yet unworthy to behold Him; but soon thou shalt see Him in all His glorious splendor, and thou wilt say, 'He alone is to be adored.' But now, if He had not placed His gentle hands before my eyes, O Thaïs, I should perhaps have fallen into sin with thee, for of myself I am but weak and sinful. But He saved us both. He is as good as He is powerful, and His name is the Savior. He was promised to the world, by David and the prophets, worshipped in His cradle by the shepherds and the magi, crucified by the Pharisees, buried by the holy women, revealed to the world by the apostles, testified to by the martyrs. And now, having learned that thou fearest death, O woman, He has come to thy house to prevent thee from dying. Art Thou not here present with me, Jesus, at this moment, as Thou didst appear to the men of Galilee, in those wonderful days when the stars, which came down with thee from heaven, were so near the earth that the holy innocents could take them in their hands, when they played in their mothers' arms on the terraces of Bethlehem? Is it not true, Jesus, that Thou art here present, and that Thou showest me in reality Thy precious body? Is not Thy face here, and that tear which flows down Thy cheek a real tear? Yes, the angel of eternal justice shall receive it, and it shall be the ransom of the soul of Thaïs. Art Thou not here, Jesus? Jesus, Thy loving lips open. Thou canst speak; speak, I hear Thee! And thee, Thaïs, happy Thaïs! listen to what the Savior Himself says to thee; it is He who speaks, not I. He says, 'I have sought thee long, O My lost sheep! I have found thee at last! Fly from Me no more. Let Me take thee by the hands, poor little one, and I will bear thee on My shoulders to the heavenly fold. Come, My Thaïs! come, My chosen one! come, and weep with Me!'"

And Paphnutius fell on his knees, his eyes filled with ecstasy. And then Thaïs saw in his face the likeness of the living Christ.

"O vanished days of my childhood!" she sobbed. "O sweet father Ahmes! good Saint Theodore, why did I not die in thy white mantle whilst thou didst bear me, in the first dawn of day, yet fresh from the waters of baptism!"

Paphnutius advanced towards her, crying —

"Thou art baptised! O divine wisdom! O Providence! O great God! I know now the power which drew me to thee. I know what rendered thee so dear and so beautiful in my eyes. It was the virtue of the baptismal water, which made me leave the shadow of God, where I lived, to seek thee in the poisoned air where men dwell. A drop — a drop, no doubt, of the water which washed thy body — has been sprinkled in my face. Come, O my sister, and receive from thy brother the kiss of peace."

And the monk touched with his lips the forehead of the courtesan.

Then he was silent, letting God speak, and nothing was heard in the Grotto of Nymphs but the sobs of Thaïs, mingled with the rippling of the running water.

She wept without trying to stop her tears, when two black slaves appeared, loaded with stuffs, perfumes, and garlands.

"It was hardly the right time to weep," she said, trying to smile. "Tears redden the eyes and spoil the complexion, and I must sup tonight with some friends, and want to be beautiful, for there will be women there quick to spy out marks of care on my face. These slaves come to dress me. Withdraw, my father, and allow them to do their work. They are clever and experienced, and I pay them well for their services. You see that one who wears thick rings of gold, and shows such white teeth. I took her from the wife of the pro-consul."

Paphnutius had at first a thought of dissuading Thaïs, as earnestly as he could, from going to this supper. But he determined to act prudently, and asked what persons she would meet there.

She replied that there would be the host, old Cotta, the Prefect of the Fleet, Nicias, and several other philosophers who loved an argument, the poet Callicrates, the high priest of Serapis, some young men whose chief amusement was training horses, and lastly some women, of whom there was little to be said except that they were young. Then, by a supernatural inspiration —

"Go amongst them, Thaïs," said the monk. "Go! But I will not leave thee. I will go with thee to this banquet, and will remain by thy side without saying a word."

She burst out laughing. And whilst her two black slaves were busy dressing her, she cried —

"What will they say when they see that I have a monk of the Thebaid for my lover?"

The Banquet

When, followed by Paphnutius, Thaïs entered the banqueting-room, the guests were already, for the most part, assembled, and reclining on their couches before the horseshoe table, which was covered with glittering vessels. In the center of the table stood a silver basin, surmounted by four figures of satyrs, who poured out from wine-skins on the boiled fish a kind of pickle in which they floated. When Thaïs appeared, acclamations arose from all sides.

Greetings to the sister of the Graces!

To the silent Melpomene, who can express all things with her looks!

Salutation to the well-beloved of gods and men!

To the much desired!

To her who gives suffering and its cure!

To the pearl of Racotis!

To the rose of Alexandria!

She waited impatiently till this torrent of praise had passed, and then said to Cotta, the host —

"Lucius, I have brought you a monk of the desert, Paphnutius, the Abbot of Antinoë. He is a great saint, whose words burn like fire."

Lucius Aurelius Cotta, the Prefect of the Fleet, rose, and replied —

"You are welcome, Paphnutius, you who profess the Christian faith. I myself have some respect of a religion that has now become imperial. The divine Constantine has placed your co-religionists in the front rank of the friends of the empire. Latin wisdom ought, in fact, to admit your Christ into our pantheon. It was a maxim of our forefathers that there was something divine in every god. But no more of that. Let us drink and enjoy ourselves while there is yet time."

Old Cotta spoke tranquilly. He had just studied a new model for a galley, and had finished the sixth book of his history of the Carthaginians. He felt sure he had not lost his day, and was satisfied with himself and the gods.

"Paphnutius," he added, "you see here several men who are worthy to be loved — Hermodorus, the High Priest of Serapis; the philosophers Dorion, Nicias, and Zenothemis; the poet Callicrates; young Chereas and young Aristobulus, both sons of dear old comrades; and near them Philina and Drosea, who deserve to be praised for their beauty."

Nicias embraced Paphnutius, and whispered in his ear —

"I warned you, brother, that Venus was powerful. It is her gentle force that has brought you here in spite of yourself. Listen: you are a man full of piety, but if you do not confess that she is the mother of the gods, your ruin is certain. Do you know that the old mathematician, Melanthes, used to say, 'I cannot demonstrate the properties of a triangle without the aid of Venus'?"

Dorion, who had for some seconds been looking at the newcomer, suddenly clapped his hands and uttered a cry of surprise.

"It is he, friends! His look, his beard, his tunic — it

is he himself! I met him at the theatre whilst our Thaïs was acting. He was furiously excited, and spoke with violence, as I can testify. He is an honest man, but he will abuse us all; his eloquence is terrible. If Marcus is the Plato of the Christians, Paphnutius is the Demosthenes. Epicurus, in his little garden, never heard the like."

Philina and Drosea, however, devoured Thaïs with their eyes. She wore on her fair hair a wreath of pale violets, each flower of which recalled, in a paler hue, the color of her eyes, so that the flowers looked like softened glances, and the eyes like sparkling flowers. It was the peculiar gift of this woman; on her everything lived, and was soul and harmony. Her robe, which was of mauve spangled with silver, trailed in long folds with a grace that was almost melancholy and was not relieved by either bracelets or necklaces. The chief charm of her appearance was her beautiful bare arms. The two friends were obliged to admire, in spite of themselves the robe and head-dress of Thaïs, though they said nothing to her on the subject.

"How beautiful you are!" said Philina. "You could not have been more so when you came to Alexandria. Yet my mother, who remembers seeing you then, says there were few women who were worthy to be compared with you."

"Who is the new lover you have brought?" asked Drosea. "He has a strange, wild appearance. If there are shepherds of elephants, assuredly he must resemble one. Where did you find such a wild-looking friend, Thaïs? Was it amongst the troglodytes who live under the earth, and are grimy with the smoke of Hades?"

But Philina put her finger on Drosea's lips.

"Hush! the mysteries of love must remain secret, and it is forbidden to know them. For my own part, certainly, I would rather be kissed by the mouth of smoking Etna than by the lips of that man. But our dear

Thaïs, who is beautiful and adorable as the goddesses, should, like the goddesses, grant all requests, and not, like us, only those of nice young men."

"Take care, both of you!" replied Thaïs. "He is a mage and an enchanter. He hears words that are whispered, and even thoughts. He will tear out your heart while you are asleep, and put a sponge in its place, and the next day, when you drink water, you will be choked to death."

She watched them grow pale, then she turned away from them, and sat on a couch by the side of Paphnutius. The voice of Cotta, kind but imperious, was suddenly heard above the murmur of conversation.

"Friends, let each take his place! Slaves, pour out the honeyed wine!"

Then, the host raising his cup —

"Let us first drink to the divine Constantine and the genius of the empire. The country should be put first of all, even above the gods, for it contains them all."

All the guests raised their full cups to their lips. Paphnutius alone did not drink, because Constantine had persecuted the Nicaean faith, and because the country of the Christian is not of this world.

Dorion, having drunk, murmured —

"What is one's country? A flowing river. The shores change, and the waves are incessantly renewed."

"I know, Dorion," replied the Prefect of the Fleet, "that you care little for the civic virtues, and you think that the sage ought to hold himself aloof from all affairs. I think, on the contrary, that an honest man should desire nothing better than to fill a responsible post in the State. The State is a noble thing."

Hermodorus, the High Priest of Serapis, spoke next —

"Dorion has asked, 'What is one's country?' I will reply that the altars of the gods and the tombs of ancestors make one's country. A man is a fellow-citizen by association of memories and hopes."

Young Aristobulus interrupted Hermodorus.

"By Castor! I saw a splendid horse today. It belonged to Demophoon. It has a fine head, small jaw, and strong forelegs. It carries its neck high and proud, like a cock."

But young Chereas shook his head.

"It is not such a good horse as you say, Aristobulus. Its hoofs are thin, and the pasterns are too low; the animal will soon go lame."

They were continuing their dispute, when Drosea uttered a piercing shriek.

"Oh! I nearly swallowed a fish-bone, as long and much sharper than a style. Luckily, I was able to get it out of my throat in time! The gods love me!"

"Did you say, Drosea, that the gods loved you?" asked Nicias, smiling. "Then they must share the same infirmities as men. Love presupposes unhappiness on the part of whoever suffers from it, and is a proof of weakness. The affection they feel for Drosea is a great proof of the imperfection of the gods."

At these words Drosea flew into a great rage.

"Nicias, your remarks are foolish and not to the point. But that is your character — you never under-stand what is said, and reply in words devoid of sense."

Nicias smiled again.

"Talk away, talk away, Drosea. Whatever you say, we are glad every time you open your mouth. Your teeth are so pretty!"

At that moment, a grave-looking old man, negli-gently dressed, walking slowly, with his head high, entered the room, and gazed at the guests quietly. Cotta made a sign to him to take a place by his side, on the same couch.

"Eucrites," he said, "you are welcome. Have you composed a new treatise on philosophy this month? That would make, if I calculate correctly, the ninety-second that has proceeded from the Nile reed you direct with an Attic hand."

Eucrites replied, stroking his silver beard —

"The nightingale was created to sing, and I was created to praise the immortal gods."

DORION. Let us respectfully salute, in Eucrites, the last of the stoics. Grave and white, he stands in the midst of us like the image of an ancestor. He is solitary amidst a crowd of men, and the words he utters are not heard.

EUCRITES. You deceive yourself, Dorion. The philosophy of virtue is not dead. I have numerous disciples in Alexandria, Rome, and Constantinople. Many of the slaves, and some of the nephews of Cæsar, now know how to govern themselves, to live independently, and being unconcerned with all affairs, they enjoy boundless happiness. Many of them have revived, in their own person, Epictetus and Marcus Aurelius. But if it were true that virtue were for ever extinguished upon the earth, in what way would the loss of it affect my happiness, since it did not depend on me whether it existed or perished? Only fools, Dorion, place their happiness out of their own power. I desire nothing that the gods do not wish, and I desire all that they do wish. By that means I render myself like unto them, and share their infallible content. If virtue perishes, I consent that it should perish, and that consent fills me with joy, as the supreme effort of my reason or my courage. In all things my wisdom will copy the divine wisdom, and the copy will be more valuable than the model; it will have cost greater care and more work.

NICIAS. I understand. You put yourself on the same level as divine providence. But if virtue consists only in effort, Eucrites, and in that intense application by which the disciples of Zeno pretend to render themselves equal to the gods, the frog, which swelled itself out to try and become as big as the ox, accomplished a masterpiece of stoicism.

EUCRITES. You jest, Nicias, and, as usual, you excel in ridicule. But if the ox of which you speak is really a god, like Apis, or like that subterranean ox whose high priest I see here, and if the frog, being wisely inspired, succeed in equaling it, would it not be, in fact, more virtuous than the ox, and could you refrain from admiring such a courageous little animal!

Four servants placed on the table a wild pig, still covered with its bristles. Little pigs, made of pastry, surrounded the animal, as though they would suckle, to show that it was a sow.

Zenothemis, turning towards the monk, said —

"Friends, a guest has come hither to join us. The illustrious Paphnutius, who leads such an extraordinary life of solitude, is our unexpected guest."

COTTA. You may even add, Zenothemis, that the place of honor is due to him, because he came without being invited.

ZENOTHEMIS. Therefore, we ought, my dear Lucius, to make him the more welcome, and strive to do that which would be most agreeable to him. Now it is certain that such a man cares less for the perfumes of meat than for the perfumes of fine thoughts. We shall, doubtless, please him by discussing the doctrine he professes, which is that of Jesus crucified. For my own part, I shall the more willingly discuss this doctrine, because it keenly interests me, on account of the number and the diversity of the allegories it contains. If one may guess at the spirit by the letter, it is filled with truths, and I consider that the Christian books abound in divine revelations. But I should not, Paphnutius, grant equal merit to the Jewish books. They were inspired not, as it was said, by the Spirit of God, but by an evil genius. Iaveh, who dictated them, was one of those spirits who people the lower air, and cause the greater part of the evils, from which we suffer; but he surpassed all the others in ignorance and ferocity. On the contrary, the serpent with golden wings, which twined its azure coils round the tree of knowledge, was made up of light and love. A combat between these two powers — the one of light and the other of darkness — was, therefore, inevitable. It occurred soon after the creation of the world. God had hardly begun to rest after His labors; Adam and Eve, the first man and the first woman, lived happy and naked in the Garden of Eden, when Iaveh conceived — to their misfortune — the design of governing them and all the generations which Eve already bore in her splendid loins. As he possessed neither the compass nor the lyre, and was equally ignorant of the science which commands and the art which persuades, he frightened these two poor children by hideous apparitions, capricious threats, and thunder-bolts. Adam and Eve, feeling his shadow upon them, pressed closer to one another, and their love waxed stronger in fear. The serpent took pity on them, and determined to instruct them, in order that, possessing knowledge, they might no longer be misled by lies. Such an undertaking required extreme prudence, and the frailty of the first human couple rendered it almost hopeless. The well-intentioned demon essayed it, however. Without the knowledge of Iaveh — who pretended to see everything, but, in reality, was not very sharp-sighted — he approached these two beings, and charmed their eyes by the splendor of his coat and the brilliancy of his wings. Then he interested their minds by forming before them, with his body, definite figures, such as the circle, the ellipse, and the spiral, the wonderful properties of which have since been recognized by the Greeks. Adam meditated on these figures more than Eve did. But when the serpent began to speak, and taught the most sublime truths — those which cannot be demonstrated — he found that Adam being made of red earth, was of too dull a nature to understand these subtle distinctions, but that Eve, on the contrary, being more tender and more sensitive, was easily impressed. Therefore he conversed with her alone, in the absence of her husband, in order to initiate her first —

DORION. Permit me, Zenothemis, to interrupt you. I speedily recognized in the myth you have explained to us an episode in the war of Pallas Athene against the giants. Iaveh much resembles Typhoon, and Pallas is represented by the Athenians with a serpent at her side. But what you have said causes me considerable doubt as to the intelligence or good faith of the serpent of whom you have spoken. If he had really possessed knowledge, would he have entrusted it to a woman's little head, which was incapable of containing it? I should rather consider that he was like Iaveh, ignorant and a liar, and that he chose Eve because she was easily seduced, and he imagined that Adam would have more intelligence and perception.

ZENOTHEMIS. Learn, Dorion, that it is not by perception and intelligence, but by sensibility, that the highest and purest truths are reached. That is why women, who, generally, are less reflective but more sensitive than men, rise more easily to the knowledge of things divine. In them is the gift of prophecy, and it is not without reason that Apollo Citharedes, and Jesus of Nazareth, are sometimes represented clad, like women, in flowing robes. The initiator was therefore wise — whatever you may say to the contrary, Dorion — in bestowing light, not on the duller Adam, but on Eve, who was whiter than milk or the stars. She freely listened to him, and allowed herself to be led to the tree of knowledge, the branches of which rose to heaven, and which was bathed with the divine spirit as with a dew. This tree was covered with leaves which spoke all the languages of future races of men, and their united voices formed a perfect harmony. Its abun-

dant fruit gave to the initiated who tasted it the knowledge of metals, stones, and plants, and also of physical
and moral laws; but this fruit was like fire, and those
who feared suffering and death did not dare to put it
to their lips. Now, as she had listened attentively to the
lessons of the serpent, Eve despised these empty terrors,
and wished to taste the fruit which gave the knowledge
of God. But, as she loved Adam, and did not wish him
to be inferior to her, she took him by the hand and
led him to the wonderful tree. Then she picked one of
the burning apples, bit it, and proffered it to her
companion. Unfortunately, Iaveh, who was by chance
walking in the garden, surprised them, and seeing that
they had become wise, he fell into a most ungovernable
rage. It is in his jealous fits that he is most to be feared.
Assembling all his forces, he created such a turmoil in
the lower air that these two weak beings were terrified.
The fruit fell from the man's hand, and the woman,
clinging to the neck of her luckless husband, said, "I
too will be ignorant and suffer with him." The trium-
phant Iaveh kept Adam and Eve and all their seed in
a condition of hebetude and terror. His art, which
consisted only in being able to make huge meteors,
triumphed over the science of the serpent, who was a
musician and geometrician. He made men unjust,
ignorant, and cruel, and caused evil to reign in the
earth. He persecuted Cain and his sons because they
were skilful workmen; he exterminated the Philistines
because they composed Orphic poems, and fables like
those of Æsop. He was the implacable enemy of science
and beauty, and for long ages the human race expiated,
in blood and tears, the defeat of the winged serpent.
Fortunately, there arose among the Greeks learned
men, such as Pythagoras, and Plato, who recovered by
the force of genius, the figures and the ideas which the
enemy of Iaveh had vainly tried to teach the first
woman. The soul of the serpent was in them; and that

is why the serpent, as Dorion has said, is honored by the Athenians. Finally, in these latter days, there appeared, under human form, three celestial spirits — Jesus of Galilee, Basilides, and Valentinus — to whom it was given to pluck the finest fruits of that tree of knowledge, whose roots pass through all the earth, and whose top reaches to the highest heaven. I have said all this in vindication of the Christians, to whom the errors of the Jews are too often imputed.

DORION. If I understood you aright, Zenothemis, you said that three wonderful men — Jesus, Basilides, and Valentinus — had discovered secrets which had remained hidden from Pythagoras and Plato, and all the philosophers of Greece, and even from the divine Epicurus, who, however, has freed men from the dread of empty terrors. You would greatly oblige me by telling me by what means these three mortals acquired knowledge which had eluded the most contemplative sages.

ZENOTHEMIS. Must I repeat to you, Dorion, that science and cogitation are but the first steps to knowledge, and that ecstasy alone leads to eternal truth?

HERMODORUS. It is true, Zenothemis, that the soul is nourished on ecstasy, as the cicada is nourished on dew. But we may even say more: the mind alone is capable of perfect rapture. For man is of a threefold nature, composed of material body, of a soul which is more subtle, but also material, and of an incorruptible mind. When, emerging from the body as from a palace suddenly given over to silence and solitude and flying through the gardens of the soul, the mind diffuses itself in God, it tastes the delights of an anticipated death, or rather of a future life, for to die is to live; and in that condition, partaking of divine purity, it possesses both infinite joy and complete knowledge. It enters into the unity which is All. It is perfected.

NICIAS. That is very fine; but, to say the truth, Hermodorus, I do not see much difference between All and Nothing. Words even seem to fail to make the distinction. Infinity is terribly like nothingness — they are both inconceivable to the mind. In my opinion perfection costs too dear; we pay for it with all our being, and to possess it must cease to exist. That is a calamity from which God Himself is not free, for the philosophers are doing their best to perfect Him. After all, if we do not know what it is *not* to be, we are equally ignorant what it is to *be*. We know nothing. It is said that it is impossible for men to agree on this question. I believe — in spite of our noisy disputes — that it is, on the contrary, impossible for men not to become some day all at unity buried under the mass of contradictions, a Pelion on Ossa, which they themselves have raised.

COTTA. I am very fond of philosophy, and study it in my leisure time. But I never understand it well, except in Cicero's books. Slaves, pour out the honeyed wine!

CALLICRATES. It is a singular thing, but when I am hungry I think of the time when the tragic poets sat at the boards of good tyrants, and my mouth waters. But when I have tasted the excellent wine that you give us so abundantly, generous Lucius, I dream of nothing but civil wars and heroic combats. I blush to live in such inglorious times; I invoke the goddess of Liberty; and I pour out my blood — in imagination — with the last Romans on the field of Philippi.

COTTA. In the days of the decline of the Republic my ancestors died with Brutus — for liberty. But there is reason to suspect that what the Roman people called liberty was only in reality the right to govern themselves. I do not deny that liberty is the greatest boon a nation can have. But the longer I live the more I am persuaded that only a strong government can bestow it on the citizens. For forty years I have filled high positions in the State, and my long experience has shown me that when the ruling power is weak the people are oppressed. Those, therefore, who — like the great majority of rhetoricians — try to weaken the government, commit an abominable crime. An autocrat, who governs by his single will, may sometimes cause most deplorable results; but if he governs by popular consent there is no remedy possible. Before the majesty of the Roman arms had bestowed peace upon all the world, the only nations which were happy were those which were ruled over by intelligent despots.

HERMODORUS. For my part, Lucius, I believe that there is no such thing as a good form of government, and that we shall never discover one, because the Greeks, who had so many excellent ideas, were never able to find one. In that respect, therefore, all hope of ultimate success is taken from us. Unmistakable signs show that the world is about to fall into ignorance and barbarism. It has been our lot, Lucius, to witness terrible events. Of all the mental satisfactions which intelligence, learning, and virtue can give, all that remains is the cruel pleasure of watching ourselves die.

COTTA. It is true that the rapacity of the people, and the boldness of the barbarians, are threatening evils. But with a good fleet, a good army, and plenty of money —

HERMODORUS. What is the use of deceiving ourselves? The dying empire will become an easy prey to the barbarians. Cities which were built by Hellenic genius, or Latin patience, will soon be sacked by drunken savages. Neither art nor philosophy will exist any longer on the earth. The statues of the gods will be overturned in the temples, and in men's hearts as well. Darkness will overcome all minds, and the world will die. Can we believe that the Sarmatians will ever devote themselves to intelligent work, that the Germani will cultivate music and philosophy, and that the Quadi and the Marcomani will adore the immortal gods? No! we are sliding toward the abyss. Our old Egypt, which was the cradle of the world, will be its burial vault; Serapis, the god of Death, will receive the last adoration of mortals, and I shall have been the last priest of the last god.

At this moment a strange figure raised the tapestry, and the guests saw before them a little hunchback, whose bald skull rose in a point. He was clad, in the Asiatic fashion, in a blue tunic, and wore round his legs, like the barbarians, red breeches, spangled with gold stars. On seeing him, Paphnutius recognized Marcus the Arian, and fearing lest a thunderbolt should fall from heaven, he covered his head with his arms, and grew pale with fright. At this banquet of the demons, neither the blasphemies of the pagans, nor the horrible errors of the philosophers, had had any effect on him, but the mere presence of the heretic quenched his courage. He would have fled, but his eyes met those of Thaïs, and he felt at once strengthened. He read in her soul that she, who was predestined to become a saint, already protected him. He seized the skirt of her long, flowing robe, and inwardly prayed to the Savior Jesus.

A murmur of acclamation welcomed the arrival of the personage who had been called the Christian Plato. Hermodorus was the first to speak.

"Most illustrious Marcus, we rejoice to see you amongst us, and it may be said that you come at the right moment. We know nothing of the Christian doctrine, beyond what is publicly taught. Now, it is certain that a philosopher, like you, cannot think as the vulgar think, and we are curious to know your opinion of the principal mysteries of the religion you profess. Our dear friend, Zenothemis, who, as you know, is always hunting for symbolic meanings, just now questioned the illustrious Paphnutius concerning the Jewish books. But Paphnutius made no reply, and we should not be surprised at that, as our guest has made a vow of silence, and God has sealed his tongue in the desert. But you Marcus, who have spoken at the Christian synods, and even at the councils of the divine Constantine, can if you wish, satisfy our curiosity by revealing to us the philosophic truths which are wrapped up in the Christian fables. Is not the first of these truths the existence of an only God — in whom, for my part, I fervently believe?"

MARCUS. Yes, venerable brethren, I believe in an only God, not begotten — the only Eternal, the origin of all things.

NICIAS. We know, Marcus, that your God created the world. That must certainly have been a great crisis in His existence. He had already existed an eternity before He could make up His mind to it. But I must, in justice, confess that His situation was a most difficult one. He must continue inactive if He would remain perfect, and must act if He would prove to Himself His own existence. You assure me that He decided to act. I am willing to believe you, although it was an unpardonable imprudence on the part of a perfect God. But tell us, Marcus, how He set about making the world.

MARCUS. Those who, without being Christians, possess, like Hermodorus and Zenothemis, the principles of knowledge, are aware that God did not create the world personally without an intermediary. He gave birth to an only Son, by whom all things were made.

HERMODORUS. That is quite true, Marcus; and this Son is worshipped under the various names of Hermes, Mithra, Adonis, Apollo, and Jesus.

MARCUS. I should not be a Christian if I gave Him any other names than those of Jesus Christ, and Savior. He is the true Son of God. But He is not eternal, since He had a beginning; as to thinking that He existed before He was begotten, we must leave that absurdity to the Nicæan mules, and the obstinate ass who too long governed the Church of Alexandria under the accursed name of Athanasius.

At these words Paphnutius, white with horror and his face bedewed with the sweat of agony made the sign of the cross, but maintained a sublime silence.

Marcus continued —

"It is clear that the foolish Nicene Creed is a treason against the majesty of the only God, by compelling Him to share His indivisible attributes with His own emanation — the Mediator by whom all things were made. Cease jesting at the true God of the Christians, Nicias, and learn that, like the lilies of the field, He toils not, neither does He spin. It was not He who was the worker, it was His only Son, Jesus, who, having created the world, came afterwards to repair His handiwork. For the creation could not be perfect, and evil was necessarily mingled with good.

NICIAS. What is "good," and what is "evil?"

There was a moment's silence, during which Hermodorus, his arm extended on the cloth, pointed to a little ass in Corinthian metal which bore two baskets — the one containing white olives, the other black olives.

"You see these olives," he said. "The contrast between the colors is pleasant to the eye, and we are content that these should be light and those should be dark. But, if they were endowed with thought and knowledge, the white would say, It is good for an olive to be white, it is bad for it to be black; and the black olives would hate the white olives. We judge better, for we are as much above them as the gods are above us. For man, who only sees a part of things, evil is an evil; for God, who understands all things, evil is a good. Doubtless ugliness is ugly, and not beautiful; but if all were beautiful, the whole would not be beautiful. It is, then, well that there should be evil, as the second Plato, far greater than the first, has demonstrated."

EUCRITES. Let us talk more morally. Evil is an evil — not for the world, of which it cannot destroy the indestructible harmony but for the sinner who does it, and cannot help doing it.

COTTA. By Jupiter! that is a good argument.

EUCRITES. The world is a tragedy by an excellent poet. God, who composed it, has intended each of us to play a part in it. If he wills that you shall be a beggar, a prince, or a cripple, make the best of the part assigned you.

NICIAS. Assuredly it would be well that the cripple should limp like Hephaistos: it would be well that the madman should indulge in all the fury of Ajax, that the incestuous woman should repeat the crimes of Phædra, that the traitor should betray, that the rascal should lie, and the murderer kill, and when the piece was played, all the actor-kings, just men, bloody tyrants, pious virgins, immodest wives, noble-minded citizens, and cowardly assassins — should receive from the poet an equal share in the felicitations.

EUCRITES. You distort my thought, Nicias, and change a beautiful young girl into a hideous Gorgon. I am sorry for you, if you are so ignorant of the nature of the gods, of justice, and of the eternal laws.

ZENOTHEMIS. For my part, friends, I believe in the reality of good and evil. But I am convinced that there is not a single human action — were it even the kiss of Judas — which does not bear within itself the germ of redemption. Evil contributes to the ultimate salvation of men, and, in that respect issues from Good, and shares the merits belonging to Good. This has been admirably expressed by the Christians, in the myth concerning the man with red hair, who, in order to betray his master, gave him the kiss of peace, and by such act assured the salvation of men. Therefore, nothing is, in my opinion, more unjust and absurd than the hate with which certain disciples of Paul, the

tentmaker, pursue the most unfortunate of the apostles
of Jesus without realizing that the kiss of Iscariot —
prophesied by Jesus Himself — was necessary, according to their own doctrine, for the redemption of men,
and that if Judas had not received the thirty pieces, the
divine wisdom would have been impugned, Providence frustrated, its designs upset, and the world given
over to evil, ignorance, and death.

MARCUS. Divine wisdom foresaw that Judas,
though he was not obliged to give the traitor's kiss,
would give it, notwithstanding. It thus employed the
sin of Iscariot as a stone in the marvelous edifice of
the redemption.

ZENOTHEMIS. I spoke just now, Marcus, as
though I believed that the redemption of men had been
accomplished by Jesus crucified, because I know that
such is the belief of the Christians, and I borrowed
their opinion that I might the better show the mistake
of those who believe in the eternal damnation of Judas.
But, in reality, Jesus was, in my eyes, but the precursor
of Basilides and Valentinus. As to the mystery of the
redemption, I will tell you, my dear friends — if you
are at all curious to hear it — how it was really accomplished on earth.

The guests made a sign of assent. Like the Athenian
virgins with the baskets sacred to Ceres, twelve young
girls, bearing on their heads baskets filled with pomegranates and apples, entered the room with a light step,
in time to the music of an invisible flute. They placed
the baskets on the table, the flute ceased, and Zenothemis spoke as follows —

"When Eunoia, 'the thought of God,' had created
the world, she confided the government of the earth
to the angels. But they did not preserve the dispassion
befitting masters. Seeing that the daughters of men
were fair, they surprised them in the evening by the
well side, and united themselves to them. From these

unions sprang a turbulent race, who covered the earth with injustice and cruelty, and the dust of the roads drank up the blood of the innocent. The sight of this caused Eunoia infinite grief.

" 'See what I have done!' she sighed, leaning towards the world. 'My poor children are plunged in misery, and by my fault. Their suffering is my crime, and I will expiate it. God Himself, who only thinks through me, would be powerless to restore them to their pristine purity. That which is done is done, and the creation will remain for ever imperfect. But, at least, I will not forsake my creatures. If I cannot make them happy, like me, I can make myself unhappy, like them. Since I committed the mistake of giving them bodies which dishonor them, I will myself assume a body like unto theirs, and will go and live amongst them.'

"Having thus spoken, Eunoia descended to the earth, and was incarnate in the breast of a woman of Argos. She was born small and feeble, and received the name of Helen. She submitted to all the labors of this life, but soon grew in grace and beauty, and became the most desired of women, as she had determined, in order that her mortal body might be tried by the most supreme defilements. An inert prey to lascivious and violent men, she suffered rape and adultery, in expiation of all the adulteries, all the violences, all the iniquities, and caused, by her beauty, the ruin of nations, that God might pardon the sins of the universe. And never was the celestial thought, never was Eunoia, so adorable as in those days when, as a woman, she prostituted herself to heroes and shepherds. The poets surmised her divinity when they painted her so peaceful, superb, and fatal, and when they addressed that invocation to her, 'A soul as serene as a calm upon the waters.'

"Thus was Eunoia led by pity into evil and suffering. She died, and the Argives still show her tomb — for it was necessary that she should know death after lust, and taste the bitter fruit she had sown. But, emerging from the decomposed flesh of Helen, she became incarnate again as a woman, and again suffered every form of insult and outrage. Thus, passing from body to body, throughout all the evil ages, she takes upon her the sins of the world. Her sacrifice will not be in vain. Joined to us by the bonds of the flesh, loving us, and weeping with us, she will effect her redemption and ours, and will carry us, clinging to her white breast, into the peace of the regained paradise."

HERMODORUS. This myth was not unknown to me. I remembered having heard that, in one of her metamorphoses, the divine Helen lived with the magician, Simon, in the reign of the Emperor Tiberius. I thought, however, that her perdition was involuntary, and that she was dragged down by the angels in their fall.

ZENOTHEMIS. It is true, Hermodorus, that men who were not properly initiated in the mysteries have imagined that the sad Eunoia was not a party to her own downfall. But if it were as they assert Eunoia would not be the expiating courtesan, the victim covered with stains of all sorts, the bread steeped in the wine of our shame, the pleasant offering, the meritorious sacrifice, the holocaust, the smoke of which rises to God. If they were not voluntary, there would be no merit in her sins.

CALLICRATES. Does anyone know, Zenothemis in what country, under what name, in what adorable form, this ever-renascent Helen is living now?

ZENOTHEMIS. A man would have to be very wise indeed to discover such a secret. And wisdom, Callicrates, is not given to poets, who live in the rude world of forms and amuse themselves, like children, with sounds and empty shows.

CALLICRATES. Beware of offending the gods, impious Zenothemis; the poets are dear to them. The first laws were dictated in verse by the immortals themselves, and the oracles of the gods are poems. Hymns have a pleasant sound to celestial ears. Who does not know that the poets are prophets, and that nothing is hidden from them? Being a poet myself, and crowned with Apollo's laurel, I will make known to all the last incarnation of Eunoia. The eternal Helen is close to us; she is looking at us, and we are looking at her. You see that woman reclining on the cushions of her couch — so beautiful and so contemplative — whose eyes shed tears, and whose lips abound with kisses! It is she! Lovely as in the time of Priam and the halcyon days of Asia, Eunoia is now called Thaïs.

PHILINA. What do you say, Callicrates? Our dear Thaïs knew Paris, Menelaus, and the Achaians who fought before Ilion! Was the Trojan horse big, Thaïs?

ARISTOBULUS. Who speaks of a horse?

"I have drunk like a Thracian!" cried Chereas and he rolled under the table.

Callicrates, raising his cup, cried —

"If we drink like desperate men, we die unavenged!"

Old Cotta was asleep, and his bald head nodded slowly above his broad shoulders.

For some time past Dorion had seemed to be greatly excited under his philosophic cloak. He reeled up to the couch of Thaïs.

"Thaïs, I love you, although it is unseemly in me to love a woman."

THAÏS. Why did you not love me before?

DORION. Because I had not supped.

THAÏS. But I, my poor friend, have drunk nothing but water; therefore you must excuse me if I do not love you.

Dorion did not wait to hear more, but made towards Drosea, who had made a sign to him in order to get him away from her friend. Zenothemis took the place he had left, and gave Thaïs a kiss on the mouth.

THAÏS. I thought you more virtuous.

ZENOTHEMIS. I am perfect, and the perfect are subject to no laws.

THAÏS. But are you not afraid of sullying your soul in a woman's arms?

ZENOTHEMIS. The body may yield to lust without the soul being concerned.

THAÏS. Go away! I wish to be loved with body and soul. All these philosophers are old goats.

The lamps died out one by one. The pale rays of dawn, which entered between the openings of the hangings, shone on the livid faces and swollen eyes of the guests. Aristobulus was sleeping soundly by the side of Chereas, and, in his dreams, devoting all his grooms to the ravens. Zenothemis pressed in his arms the yielding Philina; Dorion poured on the naked bosom of Drosea drops of wine, which rolled like rubies on the white breast, which was shaking with laughter, and the philosopher tried to catch these drops with his lips, as they rolled on the slippery flesh. Eucrites rose, and placing his arm on the shoulder of Nicias, led him to the end of the hall.

"Friend," he said, smiling, "if you can still think at all — of what are you thinking?"

"I think that the love of women is like a garden of Adonis."

"What do you mean by that?"

"Do you not know, Eucrites, that women make little gardens on the terraces, in which they plant boughs in clay pots in honor of the lover of Venus? These boughs flourish a little time, and then fade."

"What does that signify, Nicias? That it is foolish to attach importance to that which fades?"

"If beauty is but a shadow, desire is but a lightning flash. What madness it is, then, to desire beauty! Is it not rational, on the contrary, that that which passes should go with that which does not endure, and that the lightning should devour the gliding shadow?"

"Nicias, you seem to me like a child playing at knuckle-bones. Take my advice — be free! By liberty only can you become a man."

"How can a man be free, Eucrites, when he has a body?"

"You shall see presently, my son. Presently you will say, 'Eucrites was free.'"

The old man spoke, leaning against a porphyry pillar, his face lighted by the first rays of dawn. Hermodorus and Marcus had approached, and stood before him by the side of Nicias; and all four, regardless of the laughter and cries of the drinkers, conversed on things divine. Eucrites expresses himself so wisely and eloquently, that Marcus said —

"You are worthy to know the true God."

Eucrites replied —

"The true God is in the heart of the wise man."

Then they spoke of death.

"I wish," said Eucrites, "that it may find me occupied in correcting my faults, and attentive to all my duties. In the face of death I will raise my pure hands to heaven, and I will say to the gods, 'Your images, gods, that you have placed in the temple of my soul, I have not profaned; I have hung there my thoughts, as well as garlands, fillets, and wreaths. I have lived according to your providence. I have lived enough.'"

Thus speaking, he raised his arms to heaven, and he remained thoughtful a moment. Then he continued, with extreme joy —

"Separate thyself from life, Eucrites, like the ripe olive which falls; returning thanks to the tree which bore thee, and blessing the earth, thy nurse."

At these words, drawing from the folds of his robe a naked dagger, he plunged it into his breast.

Those who listened to him sprang forward to seize

his hand, but the steel point had already penetrated the heart of the sage. Eucrites had already entered into his rest. Hermodorus and Nicias bore the pale and bleeding body to one of the couches, amidst the shrill shrieks of the women, the grunts of the guests disturbed in their sleep, and the heavy breathing of the couples hidden in the shadow of the tapestry. Cotta, an old soldier, who slept lightly, woke, approached the corpse, examined the wound, and cried —

"Call Aristæus, my physician!"

Nicias shook his head.

"Eucrites is no more," he said. "He wished to die as others wish to love. He has, like all of us, obeyed his inexpressible desire. And, lo, now he is like unto the gods, who desire nothing."

Cotta struck his forehead.

"Die! To want to die when he might still serve the State! What nonsense!"

Paphnutius and Thaïs remained motionless and mute, side by side, their souls overflowing with disgust, horror, and hope.

Suddenly the monk seized the hand of the actress, and stepping over the drunkards, who had fallen close to the lascivious couples, and treading in the wine and blood spilt upon the floor, he led her out of the house.

The Papyrus

(resumed)

*T*he sun had risen over the city. Long colonnades stretched on both sides of the deserted street, and at the end shone the dome of Alexander's tomb. Here and there on the pavement lay broken wreaths and extinguished torches. Fresh wafts of the sea could be felt in the air. Paphnutius, with a look of disgust, tore off his rich robe and trampled the fragments under his feet.

"Thou hast heard them, my Thaïs!" he cried. "They have spat forth every sort of folly and abomination. They dragged the Divine Creator of all things down the gemonies* of the devils of hell, impudently denied the existence of Good and Evil, blasphemed Jesus, and exalted Judas. And the most infamous of all, the jackal of darkness, the stinking beast, the Arian full of cor-

---

* Steps on the Aventine Hill, leading to the Tiber, to which the bodies of executed criminals were dragged to be thrown into the river. The word is now obsolete, but was employed by Ben Jonson (Sejanus) and Massinger (The Roman Actor). — TRANS.

ruption and death, opened his mouth like a yawning sepulcher. My Thaïs, thou hast seen these filthy snails crawling towards thee and defiling thee with their sticky sweat; thou hast seen others, like brutes, sleeping under the heels of their slaves; thou hast seen them coupling like beasts on the carpet they had fouled with their vomit; thou hast seen a foolish old man shed a blood yet viler than the wine which flowed at his debauch, and at the end of the orgy throw himself in the face of the unforeseen Christ. Praise be to God! Thou hast seen error and recognized how hideous it was. Thaïs, Thaïs, Thaïs, recall to mind the follies of these philosophers, and say if thou wilt go mad with them! Remember the looks, the gestures, the laughs of their fitting companions, those two lascivious and malicious strumpets, and say if thou wilt remain like unto them."

Thaïs, her heart stirred with horror and disgust at all she had seen and heard that night, and feeling the indifference and brutality, the malicious jealousy of women, the heavy weight of useless hours, sighed.

"I am weary to death, O my father! Where shall I find rest? I feel that my face is burning, my head empty, and my arms are so tired that I should not have the strength to seize happiness were it within reach of my hand."

Paphnutius gazed at her with loving pity.

"Courage, O my sister! The hour of rest rises for thee, white and pure as the vapors thou seest rise from the gardens and waters."

They were near the house of Thaïs, and could see, above the wall, the tops of the sycamore and fir trees, which surrounded the Grotto of Nymphs, tremble in the morning breeze. In front of them was a public square, deserted, and surrounded with steles and votive statues, and having at each end a semicircular marble seat, supported by figures of monsters. Thaïs fell on one of these seats. Then, looking anxiously at the monk, she asked —

"What must I do?"

"Thou must," replied the monk, "follow Him who has come to seek thee. He will separate thee from this present life, as the vintager gathers the cluster that would have rotted on the tree, and bears it to the wine-press to change it into perfumed wine. Listen! there is, a dozen hours from Alexandria, towards the west, not far from the sea, a nunnery, the rules of which, a masterpiece of wisdom, deserve to be put in lyric verse and sung to the sound of the theorbo and tambourines. It may truly be said that the women who are there, submissive to these rules, have their feet upon earth and their faces in heaven. They desire to be poor, that Jesus may love them, modest, that He may gaze upon them; chaste that He may wed them. He visits them every day in the guise of a gardener, His feet bare, His beautiful hands open — even as He showed Himself to Mary at the entrance of the tomb. I will conduct thee this very day to this nunnery, my Thaïs, and soon, commingling with these holy women, thou wilt share in their heavenly conversation. They await thee as a sister. On the threshold of the convent, their mother, the pious Albina, will give thee the kiss of peace and will say, 'My daughter, thou art welcome!'"

The courtesan uttered a cry of amazement.

"Albina! a daughter of the Cæsars! The great niece of the Emperor Carus!"

"She herself! Albina, who, born in the purple, has donned the serge, and a daughter of the masters of this world, has risen to the rank of servant of Jesus Christ. She will be thy mother."

Thaïs rose and said —

"Take me to the house of Albina."

And Paphnutius, completing his victory —

"Surely I will conduct thee thither, and there I will

place thee in a cell, where thou shalt weep for thy sins. For it is not fitting that thou shouldst mingle with the daughters of Albina until thou art cleansed from thy sins. I will seal the door, and there, a happy prisoner, thou wilt wait in tears till Jesus Himself come, as a sign of pardon, to break the seal that I have placed. And doubt not that He will come, Thaïs, and how the flesh of thy soul will tremble when thou shalt feel the fingers of Light placed upon thy eyes to dry thy tears!"

Thaïs said a second time —

"Take me, my father, to the house of Albina."

His heart filled with joy, Paphnutius gazed around him, and tasted, almost without fear, the pleasure of contemplating the works of creation; his eyes drank in with joy God's light, and unknown breezes fanned his cheeks. Suddenly, seeing at one of the corners of the public square the little door which led to Thaïs' house, and remembering that the trees, whose foliage he had been admiring, shaded the courtesan's garden, he thought of all the impurities which there sullied the air, today so light and pure, and his soul was so grieved that bitter tears sprang to his eyes.

"Thaïs," he said, "we must fly without looking back. But we must not leave behind us the instruments, the witnesses, the accomplices of thy past crimes; those heavy hangings, those beds, carpets, perfume censers and lamps, which would proclaim thy infamy! Dost thou wish that, animated by the demons, and carried by the evil spirit that is in them, those accursed belongings should pursue thee even to the desert? It is but too true that there are tables which bring ruin, seats which serve as the instruments of devils, which act, speak, strike the ground, and pass through the air. Let all perish which has seen thy shame! Hasten, Thaïs, and, whilst the city is yet asleep, order thy slaves to make, in the center of this place, a pile, upon which we will burn all the abominable riches thy dwelling contains."

Thaïs consented.

"Do as you will, my father," she said. "I know that spirits often dwell in inanimate objects. At night some articles of furniture talk, either by giving knocks at regular intervals or by emitting little flashes of light as signals. And even more. Have you remarked, my father, at the entrance to the Grotto of Nymphs, on the right, a statue of a naked woman about to bathe? One day I saw, with my own eyes, that statue turn its head like a living person, and then return to its ordinary attitude. I was terrified. Nicias, to whom I related this prodigy, laughed at me; yet there must be some magic in that statue, for it inspired with violent desires a certain Dalmatian, who was insensible to my beauty. It is certain that I have lived amongst enchanted things, and that I was exposed to the greatest perils, for men have been strangled by the embraces of a bronze statue. Yet it would be a pity to destroy valuable works made with rare skill, and to burn my carpets and tapestry would be a great loss. The beautiful colors of some of them are truly wonderful, and they cost much money to those who gave them to me. I also possess cups, statues, and pictures of great price. I do not think they ought to perish. But you know what is necessary. Do as you will, my father."

Thus saying, she followed the monk to the little door at which so many garlands and wreaths had been hung, and, when it was opened, she told the porter to call together all the slaves in the house. Four Indians, who were employed in the kitchen, were the first to appear. They were all four yellow men, and each had but one eye. It had cost Thaïs much trouble, and given her amusement, to get together these four slaves of the same race, and all afflicted with the same infirmity. When they attended at table they excited the curiosity of the guests, and Thaïs made them relate the story of

their lives. These four waited in silence. Their assistants
followed them. Then came the stablemen, the hunts-
men, the litter-bearers, and the running footmen with
muscles like iron, two gardeners hirsute as Priapus, six
ferocious looking Negroes, three Greek slaves — one a
grammarian, another a poet, and the third a singer.
They all stood, ranged in order, on the public square,
and were presently joined by the Negresses — curious,
suspicious, rolling big round eyes, and each with a huge
mouth slit to her earrings. Lastly, adjusting their veils
and languidly dragging their feet, which were shackled
with light gold chains, appeared six sulky-looking,
beautiful white slave-girls. When they were all assembled, Thaïs, pointing to Paphnutius, said —

"Do whatever this man commands you; for the spirit
of God is in him, and if you disobey him you will fall
dead."

For she had heard, and really believed, that the earth
would open and swallow up in flames and smoke any
impious wretch whom a saint of the desert struck with
his staff.

Paphnutius sent away the women and the Greek
men-slaves, and said to the others —

"Bring wood to the middle of this place, make a huge
fire, and throw into it pell-mell all that there is in the
house and grotto."

They were astonished, and stood motionless, looking at their mistress. And they still stood inactive and
silent, and pressed against each other, elbow to elbow,
suspecting that the order was a joke.

"Obey!" said the monk.

Several of them were Christians. They understood
the command, and went to the house to fetch wood
and torches. The others were not indisposed to imitate
them, for, being poor, they hated riches and had a
natural instinct for destruction. Whilst they were
building the pile, Paphnutius said to Thaïs —

"I thought at one time of fetching the treasurer of one of the churches of Alexandria (if there still remain one worthy of the name of church, and that is not defiled by the Arian beasts) and giving him thy goods, woman, that he might distribute them to widows, and change the proceeds of crime into the treasure of justice. But such a thought did not come from God, and I cast it from me, for assuredly it would be a great offence to the well-beloved of Jesus Christ to offer them the spoils of thy lust. Thaïs, all that thou hast touched must be devoured by the fire, even to its very soul. Thanks be to Heaven, these tunics and veils, which have seen kisses more innumerable than the waves of the sea, will only feel now the lips and tongues of the flames. Hasten, slaves! More wood! More links and torches! And thou, woman, return to thy house, strip thyself of thy shameful robes, and ask of the most humble of thy slaves, as an undeserving favor, the tunic that she puts on when she scrubs the floors."

Thaïs obeyed. Whilst the Indians knelt down and blew the embers, the Negroes threw on the pile coffers of ivory, ebony, or cedar, which broke open and let out wreaths, garlands, and necklaces. The smoke rose in a dark column, as in the holocausts of the old religion. Then the fire, which had been smoldering, burst out suddenly with a roar as of some monstrous animal, and the almost invisible flames began to devour their valuable prey. The slaves worked more eagerly; they joyfully dragged out rich carpets, veils embroidered with silver, and flowered tapestry. They staggered under the weight of tables, couches, thick cushions, and beds with gold nails. Three strong Ethiopians came hugging the colored statues of the nymphs, one of which had been loved as though it were a mortal; and they looked like huge apes carrying off women. And when the beautiful naked forms fell from the arms of these monsters, and were broken on the stones, a deep groan was heard.

At that moment Thaïs appeared, her hair unloosed and streaming over her shoulders, barefooted, and clad in a clumsy coarse garment which seemed redolent with divine voluptuousness merely from having touched her body. Behind her came a gardener, carrying, half hidden in his long beard, an ivory Eros.

She made a sign to the man to stop, and approaching Paphnutius, showed him the little god.

"My father," she asked, "should this also be thrown into the flames? It is of marvelous antique work, and is worth a hundred times its weight in gold. Its loss would be irreparable, for there is not a sculptor in the world capable of making such a beautiful Eros. Remember also, my father, that this child is Love, and he should not be harshly treated. Believe me, Love is a virtue, and if I have sinned, it is not through him, my father, but against him. Never shall I regret aught that he has caused me to do, and I deplore only those things I have done contrary to his commands. He does not allow women to give themselves to those who do not come in his name. For that reason he ought to be honored. Look, Paphnutius, how pretty this little Eros is! With what grace he hides himself in the gardener's beard! One day Nicias, who loved me then, brought it to me and said, 'It will remind you of me.' But the roguish boy did not remind me of Nicias, but of a young man I knew at Antioch. Enough riches have been destroyed upon this pile, my father! Preserve this Eros, and place it in some monastery. Those who see it will turn their hearts towards God, for love leads naturally to heavenly thoughts."

The gardener, already believing that the little Eros was saved, smiled on it as though it had been a child, when Paphnutius, snatching the god from the arms which held it, threw it into the flames, crying —

"It is enough that Nicias has touched it to make it

replete with every sort of poison!"

Then, seizing by armfuls the sparkling robes, the purple mantles, the golden sandals, the combs, strigils, mirrors, lamps, theorbos, and lyres, he threw them into this furnace, more costly than the funeral pile of Sardanapalus, whilst, drunken with the rage of destruction, the slaves danced round, uttering wild yells amid a shower of sparks and ashes.

One by one, the neighbors, awakened by the noise, opened the windows, and rubbing their eyes, looked out to see whence the smoke came. Then they came down, half dressed, and drew near the fire.

"What does it mean?" they wondered.

Amongst them were merchants from whom Thaïs had often bought perfumes and stuffs, and they looked on anxiously with long, yellow faces, unable to comprehend what was going on. Some young debauchees, who, returning from a supper, passed by there, preceded by their slaves, stopped, their heads crowned with flowers, their tunics floating, and uttered loud cries. Attracted by curiosity, the crowd increased unceasingly, and soon it was known that Thaïs had been persuaded by the Abbot of Antinoë to burn her riches and retire to a nunnery.

The shopkeepers thought to themselves —

"Thaïs is going to leave the city; we shall sell no more to her; it is dreadful to think of. What will become of us without her? This monk has driven her mad. He is ruining us. Why let him do it? What is the use of the laws? Are there no magistrates in Alexandria? Thaïs does not think about us and our wives and our poor children. It is a public scandal. She ought to be compelled to stay in the city."

The young men, on their part, also thought —

"If Thaïs is going to renounce acting and love, our chief amusements will be taken from us. She was the glory, delight, and honor of the stage. She was the joy even of those who had never possessed her. The women we loved, we loved in her. There were no kisses given in which she was altogether absent, for she was the joy of all voluptuaries, and the mere thought that she breathed amongst us excited us to pleasure."

Thus thought the young men, and one of them, named Cerons, who had held her in his arms, cried out upon the abduction, and blasphemed against Christ. In every group the conduct of Thaïs was severely criticized.

"It is a shameful flight!"

"A cowardly desertion!"

"She is taking the bread out of our mouths."

"She is robbing our children."

"She ought at least to pay for the wreaths I have sold to her."

"And the sixty robes she has ordered of me."

"She owes money to everybody."

"Who will represent Iphigenia, Electra, and Polyxena when she is gone? The handsome Polybia herself will not make such a success as she has done."

"Life will be dull when her door is closed."

"She was the bright star, the soft moon of the Alexandrian sky."

All the most notorious mendicants of the city — cripples, blind men, and paralytics — had by this time assembled in the place; and crawling through the remnants of the riches, they groaned —

"How shall we live when Thaïs is no longer here to feed us? Every day the fragments from her table fed two hundred poor wretches, and her lovers, when they quitted her, threw us as they passed handfuls of silver pieces."

Some thieves, too, also mingled with the crowd, and created a deafening clamor, and pushed their neighbors, to increase disorder, and take advantage of the tumult to filch some valuable object.

Old Taddeus, who sold Miletan wool and Tarentan linen, and to whom Thaïs owed a large sum of money, alone remained calm and silent in the midst of the uproar. He listened and watched, and gently stroking his goat-beard, seemed thoughtful. At last he approached young Cerons, and pulling him by the sleeve, whispered —

"You are the favored lover of Thaïs, handsome youth; show yourself, and do not allow this monk to carry her off."

"By Pollux and his sister, he shall not!" cried Cerons. "I will speak to Thaïs, and without flattering myself, I think she will listen to me rather than to that sooty-faced Lapithan. Place! Place, dogs!"

And striking with his fist the men, upsetting the old women and treading on the young children, he reached Thaïs, and taking her aside —

"Dearest girl," he said, "look at me, remember, and tell me truly if you renounce love."

But Paphnutius threw himself between Thaïs and Cerons.

"Impious wretch!" he cried, "beware and touch her not; she is sacred — she belongs to God."

"Get away, baboon!" replied the young man furiously. "Let me speak to my sweetheart, or if not I will drag your obscene carcass by the beard to the fire, and roast you like a sausage."

And he put his hand on Thaïs. But, pushed away by the monk with unexpected force, he staggered back four paces and fell at the foot of the pile amongst the scattered ashes.

Old Taddeus, meanwhile, had been going from one to the other, pulling the ears of the slaves and kissing the hands of the masters, inciting each and all against Paphnutius, and had already formed a little band resolutely determined to oppose the monk who would steal Thaïs from them.

Cerons rose, his face black, his hair singed, and choking with smoke and rage. He blasphemed against the gods, and threw himself amongst the assailants, behind whom the beggars crawled, shaking their crutches. Paphnutius was soon enclosed in a circle of menacing fists, raised sticks, and cries of death.

"To the ravens with the monk! to the ravens!"

"No; throw him in the fire! Burn him alive!"

Seizing his fair prey, he pressed her to his heart.

"Impious men," he cried in a voice of thunder, "strive not to tear the dove from the eagle of the Lord. But rather copy this woman, and like she turn your filth into gold. Imitate her example, and renounce the false wealth which you think you hold and which holds you. Hasten! the day is at hand, and divine patience begins to grow weary. Repent, confess your sins, weep and pray. Walk in the footsteps of Thaïs. Hate your offenses, which are as great as hers. Which of you, poor or rich, merchants, soldiers, slaves or eminent citizens, would dare to say, before God, that he was better than a prostitute? You are all nothing but living filth, and it is by a miracle of divine goodness that you do not suddenly turn into streams of mire."

Whilst he spoke flames shot from his eyes; an it seemed as though live coals came from his lips and those who surrounded him were obliged to hear him in spite of themselves.

But old Taddeus did not remain idle. He picked up stones and oyster shells, which he hid in the skirt of his tunic, and not daring to throw them himself slipped them into the hands of the beggars. Soon the stones began to fly, and a well-directed shell cut Paphnutius' face. The blood, which flowed down the dark face of the martyr, dropped in a new baptism on the head of the penitent, and Thaïs, half stifled in the monk's embrace and her delicate skin scratched by the coarse cassock, felt a thrill of horror and fright.

At that moment a man elegantly dressed, and with a wreath of wild celery on his head, opened a road for himself through the furious crowd, and cried —

"Stop! Stop! This monk is my brother!"

It was Nicias, who, having closed the eyes of the philosopher Eucrites, was passing through the square to return to his house;. and saw, without very much surprise (for nothing astonished him), the smoking pile, Thaïs clad an a serge cassock, and Paphnutius being stoned.

He repeated —

"Stop, I tell you; spare my old fellow scholar; respect the beloved head of Paphnutius!"

But, being only used to subtle disquisitions with philosophers, he did not possess that imperious energy which commands vulgar minds. He was not listened to. A shower of stones and shells fell on the monk, who, protecting Thaïs with his body, praised the Lord whose goodness turned his wounds into caresses. Despairing of making himself heard, and feeling but too sure that he could not save his friend either by force or persuasion, Nicias resigned himself to the will of the gods — in whom he had little confidence — when the idea occurred to him to use a stratagem which his contempt for men had suddenly suggested to him. He took from his girdle his purse, which was full of gold and silver, for he was a pleasure-loving and charitable man, and running up to the men who were throwing the stones, he chinked the money in their ears. At first they paid no attention to him, their fury being too great; but little by little their looks turned towards the chinking gold, and soon their arms dropped and no longer menaced their victim. Seeing that he had attracted their eyes and minds, Nicias opened his purse and threw some pieces of gold and silver amongst the crowd. The more greedy of them stooped to pick it up. The philosopher, pleased at his first success, adroitly threw deniers and drachmas here and there. At the sound of the pieces of money rattling on the pavement, the persecutors of Paphnutius threw themselves on the ground. Beggars, slaves, and trades people scrambled after the money, whilst, grouped round Cerons, the patricians watched the struggle and laughed heartily. Cerons himself quite forgot his wrath. His friends encouraged the rivals, chose competitors, and made bets, and urged on the miserable wretches as they would have done fighting dogs. A cripple without legs having succeeded in seizing a drachma, the applause was frenetic. The young men themselves began to throw money, and nothing was to be seen in the square but a multitude of backs, rising and falling like waves of the sea, under a shower of coins. Paphnutius was forgotten.

Nicias ran up to him, covered him with his cloak, and dragged him and Thaïs into by-streets where they were safe from pursuit. They ran for some time in silence, and when they thought they were out of reach of their enemies, they ceased running, and Nicias said, in a tone of raillery in which a little sadness was mingled —

"It is finished then! Pluto ravishes Proserpine, and Thaïs will follow my fierce-looking friend whithersoever he will lead her."

"It is true, Nicias," replied Thaïs, "that I am tired of living with men like you, smiling, perfumed, kindly egoists. I am weary of all I know, and I am, therefore, going to seek the unknown. I have experienced joy that was not joy, and here is a man who teaches me that sorrow is true joy. I believe him, for he knows the truth."

"And I, sweetheart," replied Nicias, smiling, "I know the truths. He knows but one, I know them all. I am superior to him in that respect, but to tell the truth, it doesn't make me any the prouder nor any the happier."

Then, seeing that the monk was glaring fiercely at him —

"My dear Paphnutius, do not imagine that I think you extremely absurd, or even altogether unreasonable. And if I were to compare your life with mine, I could not say which is preferable in itself. I shall presently go and take the bath which Crobyle and Myrtale have prepared for me; I shall eat the wing of a Phasian pheasant; then I shall read — for the hundredth time — some fable by Apuleius or some treatise by Porphyry. You will return to your cell, where, leaning like a tame camel, you will ruminate on — I know not what — formulas of incarnations you have long chewed and rechewed, and in the evening you will swallow some radishes without any oil. Well, my dear friend, in accomplishing these acts, so different apparently, we are both obeying the same sentiment, the only motive for all human actions; we are both seeking our own pleasure, and striving to attain the same end — happiness, the impossible happiness. It would be folly on my part to say you were wrong, dear friend, even though I think myself in the right.

"And you, my Thaïs, go and enjoy yourself, and be more happy still, if it be possible, in abstinence and austerity than you have been in riches and pleasure. On the whole, I should say you were to be envied. For if in our whole lives, Paphnutius and I have pursued but one kind of pleasurable satisfaction, you in your life, dear Thaïs, have tasted diverse joys such as it is rarely given to the same person to know. I should really like to be for one hour, a saint like our dear friend Paphnutius. But that is not possible. Farewell, then, Thaïs! Go where the secret forces of nature and your destiny conduct you! Go, and take with you, whithersoever you go, the good wishes of Nicias! I know that is mere foolishness, but can I give you anything more than barren regrets and vain wishes in payment for the delicious illusions which once enveloped me when I was in your arms, and of which only the shadow now remains to me? Farewell, my benefactress! Farewell, goodness that is ignorant of its own existence, mysterious virtue, joy of men! Farewell to the most adorable of the images that nature has ever thrown — for some unknown reasons — on the face of this deceptive world!"

Whilst he spoke, deep wrath had been brewing in the monk's heart, and it now broke forth in imprecations.

"Avaunt, cursed wretch! I scorn thee and hate thee. Go, child of hell, a thousand times worse than those poor lost ones who just now threw stones and insults at me! They knew not what they did, and the grace of God, which I implored for them, may some day descend into their hearts. But thou, detestable Nicias, thou art but a perfidious venom and a bitter poison. Thy mouth breathes despair and death. One of thy smiles contains more blasphemy than issues in a century from the smoking lips of Satan. Avaunt, backslider!"

Nicias looked at him.

"Farewell, my brother," he said, "and may you preserve until your life's end your store of faith, hate, and love. Farewell, Thaïs! It is in vain that you will forget me, because I shall ever remember you."

On quitting them he walked thoughtfully through the winding streets in the vicinity of the great cemetery of Alexandria, which are peopled by the makers of funeral urns. Their shops were full of clay figures painted in bright colors and representing gods and goddesses, mimes, women, winged sprites, &c., such as were usually buried with the dead. He fancied that perhaps some of the little images which he saw there might be the companions of his eternal sleep; and it seemed to him that a little Eros, with its tunic tucked up, laughed at him mockingly. He looked forward to his death, and the idea was painful to him. To cure his sadness he tried to philosophize, and reasoned thus —

"Assuredly," he said to himself, "time has no reality. It is a simple illusion of our minds. Then, if it does not exist, how can it bring death to me? Does that mean that I shall live for ever? No, but I conclude therefrom that my death is, always has been, as it always will be. I do not feel it yet, but it is in me, and I ought not to fear it, for it would be folly to dread the coming of that which has arrived. It exists, like the last page of a book I read and have not finished."

This argument occupied him all the rest of the way, but without making him more cheerful; and his mind was filled with dismal thoughts when he arrived at the door of his house and heard the merry laughter of Crobyle and Myrtale, who were playing at tennis whilst they were waiting for him.

Paphnutius and Thaïs left the city by the Gate of the Moon, and followed the coast.

"Woman," said the monk, "all that great blue sea could not wash away thy pollutions."

He spoke with scorn and anger.

"More filthy than a bitch or a sow, thou hast prostituted to pagans and infidels a body which the Eternal had intended for a tabernacle, and thy impurities are such that, now that thou knowest the truth, thou canst not unite thy lips or join thy hands without a horror of thyself rising in thy heart."

She followed him meekly, over stony roads, under a burning sun. Her knees ached from fatigue, and her throat was parched with thirst. But, far from feeling any of the pity which softens the hearts of the profane, Paphnutius rejoiced at these propitiatory sufferings of the flesh which had so sinned. So infuriated was he with holy zeal that he would have liked to cut with rods the body that had preserved its beauty as a shining witness to its infamy. His meditations augmented his pious fury, and remembering that Thaïs had received Nicias in her bed, that idea seemed so horrible to him that his blood all flowed back to his heart, and his breast felt ready to burst. His curses were stifled in his throat, and he could only grind his teeth. He sprang forward and stood before her, pale, terrible, and filled with the Spirit of God — looked into her very soul, and then spat in her face.

She calmly wiped her face and continued to walk on. He followed, glaring at her in pious anger, as if she had been hell itself. He was thinking how he could avenge Christ in order that Christ should not avenge Himself, when he saw a drop of blood that had dripped from the foot of Thaïs on the sand. Then a hitherto unknown influence entered his opened heart, sobs rose to his lips, he wept, he ran and knelt before her, called her his sister, and kissed her bleeding feet. He murmured a hundred times, "My sister, my sister, my mother, O most holy!"

He prayed —

"Angels of heaven, receive carefully this drop of blood, and bear it before the throne of the Lord. And may a miraculous anemone blossom on the sand sprinkled with the blood of Thaïs, that those who see the flower may recover purity of heart and feeling. O holy, holy, most holy Thaïs!"

As he prayed and prophesied thus, a lad passed on an ass. Paphnutius ordered him to descend, seated Thaïs on the ass, and led it by the bridle. Towards evening they came to a canal shaded by fine trees; he tied the ass to the trunk of a date palm, and sitting on a mossy stone he shared with Thaïs a loaf, which they ate with salt and hyssop. They drank fresh water in their hands, and talked of things eternal. She said —

"I have never drunk water so pure nor breathed an air so light, and I feel that God floats in the breezes that pass."

"Look! it is the evening, O my sister. The blue shadows of night cover the hills. But soon thou wilt see shining in the dawn the tabernacles of Light; soon thou wilt behold shine forth the roses of the eternal morning."

They journeyed all night, and, while the crescent moon gleamed on the silver crests of the waves, they sang psalms and hymns. When the sun rose, the Libyan desert stretched before them like a huge lion-skin. At the edge of the desert, and close to a few palm-trees, some white huts shimmered in the morning light.

"Are those the tabernacles of Light, father?" asked Thaïs.

"Even so, my daughter and my sister. Yonder is the House of Salvation, where I will confine you with my own hands."

Soon they saw a number of women busy around the buildings, like bees round their hives. There were some who baked bread, or prepared vegetables; many were spinning wool, and the light of heaven shone upon them like a smile of God. Others meditated in the shade of the tamarisk trees; their white hands hung by their sides, for, being filled with love, they had chosen the part of Magdalen, and performed no work but prayer, contemplation, and ecstasy. They were, therefore, called the Marys, and were clad in white. Those who worked with their hands were called the Marthas, and wore blue robes. All wore the hood, but the younger ones allowed a few curls to show on their foreheads — unintentionally, it is to be presumed, since it was forbidden by the rules. A very old lady, tall and white, walked from cell to cell, leaning on a staff of hard wood. Paphnutius approached her respectfully, kissed the hem of her veil, and said —

"The peace of the Lord be with thee, venerable Albina. I have brought to the hive, of which thou art queen, a bee I found lost on a flowerless road. I took it in the palm of my hand, and revived it with my breath. I give it to thee."

And he pointed to the actress, who knelt down before the daughter of the Cæsars.

Albina cast a piercing glance on Thaïs, ordered her to rise, kissed her on the forehead, and then, turning to the monk —

"We will place her," she said, "amongst the Marys."

Paphnutius then related how Thaïs had been brought to the House of Salvation, and asked that she should be at once confined in a cell. The abbess consented, and led the penitent to a hut, which had remained empty since the death of the virgin Læta, who had sanctified it. In this narrow chamber there was but a bed, a table, and a pitcher, and Thaïs when she crossed the threshold, felt filled with ineffable joy.

"I wish to close the door myself," said Paphnutius, "and put thereon a seal, which Jesus will come and break with His own hands."

He went to the side of the spring, and took a handful of wet clay, mixed with it a little spittle and a hair from his head, and plastered it across the chink of the door. Then, approaching the window, near which Thaïs stood peaceful and happy, he fell on his knees and praised the Lord three times.

"How beautiful are the feet of her who walketh in the paths of righteousness! How beautiful are her feet, and how resplendent her face!"

He rose, lowered his hood over his eyes, and walked away slowly.

Albina called one of her virgins.

"My daughter," she said, "take to Thaïs those things which are needful for her — bread, water, and a flute with three holes."

PART
THE THIRD

The Euphorbia

*P*aphnutius had returned to the holy desert. He took, near Athribis, the boat which went up the Nile to carry food to the monastery of Abbot Serapion. When he disembarked, his disciples advanced to meet him with great demonstrations of joy. Some raised their arms to heaven; others, prostrate on the ground, kissed the Abbot's sandals. For they knew already what the saint had accomplished in Alexandria. The monks generally received, by rapid and unknown means, information concerning the safety or glory of the Church. News spread through the desert with the rapidity of the simoon.

When Paphnutius strode across the sand, his disciples followed him, praising the Lord. Flavian, who was the oldest member of the brotherhood, was suddenly seized with a pious frenzy and began to sing an inspired hymn —

"O blessed day! Now is our father restored to us.

He has returned laden with fresh merits, of which we reap the benefit.

For the virtues of the father are the wealth of the children, and the sanctity of the Abbot illuminates every cell.

Paphnutius, our father, has given a new spouse to Jesus Christ.

By his wondrous art, he has changed a black sheep into a white sheep.

And now, behold, he has returned to us, laden with fresh merits.

Like unto the bee of the Arsinoetid, heavy with the nectar of flowers.

Even as the ram of Nubia, which could hardly bear the weight of its abundant wool.

Let us celebrate this day by mingling oil with our food."

When they came to the door of the Abbot's cell, they fell on their knees, and said —

"Let our father bless us, and give each of us a measure of oil to celebrate his return."

Paul the Fool, who alone had remained standing, asked, "Who is this man?" and did not recognize Paphnutius. But no one paid any attention to what he said, as he was known to be devoid of intelligence, though filled with piety.

The Abbot of Antinoë, locked in his cell, thought —

"I have at last regained the haven of my repose and happiness. I have returned to my fortress of contentment. But how is it that this roof of rushes, so dear to me, does not receive me as a friend, and the walls say not to me, 'Thou art welcome.' Nothing has changed, since my departure, in this abode I have chosen. There is my table and my bed. There is the mummy's head which has so often inspired me with salutary thoughts;

and there is the book in which I have so often sought conceptions of God. And yet nothing that I left is here. The things appear grievously despoiled of their customary charm, and it seems to me as though I saw them today for the first time. When I look at that table and couch, that in former days I made with my own hands, that black, dried head, these rolls of papyrus filled with the sayings of God, I seem to see the belongings of a dead man. After having known them all so well, I know them no longer. Alas! since nothing around me has really changed, it is I who am no longer what I was. I am another. I am the dead man! What has happened, my God? What has been taken from me? What is left unto me? And who am I?"

And it especially perplexed him to find, in spite of himself, that his cell was small, whereas, when viewed by the eye of faith, he ought to consider it immense, because the infinitude of God began there.

He began to pray, with his face against the ground, and felt a little happier. He had hardly been an hour in prayer, when a vision of Thaïs passed before his eyes. He returned thanks to God —

"Jesus! it is Thou who hast sent her. I acknowledge in that Thy wonderful goodness; Thou wouldst please me, reassure me and comfort me by the sight of her whom I have given to Thee. Thou; presentest her to my eyes with her smile now disarmed; her grace, now become innocent; her beauty from which I have extracted the sting. To please me, my God, thou showest her to me as I have prepared and purified her for Thy designs, as one friend pleasantly reminds another of the rich gift he has received from him. Therefore I see this woman with delight, being assured that the vision comes from Thee. Thou dost not forget that I have given her to Thee, Jesus. Keep her, since she pleases Thee, and suffer not her beauty to give joy to any but Thyself."

He could not sleep all night, and he saw Thaïs more distinctly than he had seen her in the Grotto of Nymphs. He commended himself, saying —

"What I have done, I have done to the glory of God."

Yet, to his great surprise, his heart was not at ease. He sighed.

"Why art thou sad, O my soul, and why dost thou trouble me?"

And his mind was still perturbed. Thirty days he remained in that condition of sadness which precedes the sore trials of a solitary monk. The image of Thaïs never left him day or night. He did not try to banish it, because he still thought it came from God, and was the image of a saint. But one morning she visited him in a dream, her hair crowned with violets, and her very gentleness seemed so formidable, that he uttered a cry of fright, and woke in an icy sweat. His eyes were still heavy with sleep, when he felt a moist warm breath on his face. A little jackal, its two paws placed on the side of the bed, was panting its stinking breath in his face, and grinning at him.

Paphnutius was greatly astonished, and it seemed to him as though a tower had given way under his feet. And, in fact, he had fallen, for his self-confidence had gone. For some time he was incapable of thought and when he did recover himself, his meditations only increased his perplexity.

"It is one of two things," he said to himself; "either this vision, like the preceding ones, came from God, and was a good vision, and it is my natural perversity which has misrepresented it, as wine turns sour in a dirty cup. I have, by my unworthiness, changed instruction into reproach, of which this diabolical jackal immediately took advantage. Or else this vision came, not from God, but, on the contrary, from the devil, and was evil. In that case I should doubt whether the former ones had, as I thought, a celestial origin. I am therefore incapable of that discernment which is necessary for the ascetic. In either case it is plain that God is no longer with me, — of which I feel the effects, though I cannot explain the cause."

He reasoned in this way, and anxiously asked —

"Just God, what trials dost Thou appoint for Thy servants if the apparitions of Thy saints are a danger for them? Give me to discern, by an intelligible sign, that which comes from Thee, and that which comes from the other."

And as God, whose designs are inscrutable, did not see fit to enlighten his servant, Paphnutius, lost in doubt, resolved not to think of Thaïs any more. But his resolutions were vain. Though absent, she was ever with him. She gazed at him whilst he read, or meditated, or prayed, or met his eyes wherever he looked. Her imaginary approach was heralded by a slight sound, such as is made by a woman's dress when she walks, and the visions had more verisimilitude than reality itself, which moves and is confused, whereas the phantoms which are caused by solitude are fixed and unchangeable. She came under various appearances — sometimes pensive, her head crowned with her last perishable wreath, clad as at the banquet at Alexandria, in a mauve robe spangled with silver flowers; sometimes voluptuously in a cloud of light veils, and bathed in the warm shadows of the Grotto of Nymphs; sometimes in a serge cassock, pious and radiant with celestial joy; sometimes tragic, her eyes swimming in the terrors of death, and showing her bare breast bedewed with the blood from her pierced heart. What disturbed him the most in these visions was that the wreaths, tunics, and veils, that he had burned with his own hands, should thus return; it became evident to him that these things had an imperishable soul, and he cried —

"Lo, all the countless souls of the sins of Thaïs come upon me!"

When he turned away his head, he felt that Thaïs was behind him, and that made him feel still more uneasy. His torture was cruel. But as his soul and body remained pure in the midst of all his temptations, he trusted in God, and gently complained to Him.

"My God, if I went so far to seek her amongst the Gentiles, it was for Thy sake, and not for mine. It would not be just that I should suffer for what I have done in Thy behalf. Protect me, sweet Jesus! My Savior, save me! Suffer not the phantom to accomplish that which the body could not. As I have triumphed over the flesh, suffer not the shadow to overthrow me. I know that I am now exposed to greater dangers than I ever ran. I feel and know that the dream has more power than the reality. And how could it be otherwise, since it is itself but a higher reality? It is the soul of things. Plato, though he was but an idolater, has testified to the real existence of ideas. At that banquet of demons to which Thou accompaniedst me, Lord, I heard men — sullied with crimes truly, but certainly not devoid of intelligence — agree to acknowledge that we see real objects in solitude, meditation, and ecstasy; and Thy Scriptures, my God, many times affirm the virtue of dreams, and the power of visions formed either by Thee, great God, or by Thy adversary."

There was a new man in him and now he reasoned with God, but God did not choose to enlighten him. His nights were one long dream, and his days did not differ from his nights. One morning he awoke uttering sighs, such as issue, by moonlight, from the tombs of the victims of crimes. Thaïs had come, showing her bleeding feet, and whilst he wept, she had slipped into his couch. There was no longer any doubt; the image of Thaïs was an impure image.

His heart filled with disgust, he leaped out of his profaned couch, and hid his face in his hands that he might not see the daylight. The hours passed, but they did not remove his shame. All was quiet in the cell. For the first time for many long days, Paphnutius was alone. The phantom had at last left him, and even its absence seemed dreadful. Nothing, nothing to distract his mind from the recollection of the dream. Full of horror, he thought —

"Why did I not drive her away? Why did I not tear myself from her cold arms and burning knees?"

He no longer dared to pronounce the name of God near that horrible couch, and he feared that his cell being profaned, the demons might freely enter at any hour. His fears did not deceive him. The seven little jackals, which had never crossed the threshold, entered in a file, and went and hid under the bed. At the vesper hour, there came an eighth, the stench of which was horrible. The next day, a ninth joined the others, and soon there were thirty, then sixty, then eighty. They became smaller as they multiplied, and being no bigger than rats, they covered the floor, the couch, and the stool. One of them jumped on the little table by the side of the bed, and standing with its four feet together on the death's head, looked at the monk with burning eyes. And every day fresh jackals came.

To expiate the abominable sin of his dream, and flee from impure thoughts, Paphnutius determined to leave his cell, which had now become polluted, go far into the desert, and practice unheard-of austerities, strange labors, and fresh works of grace. But before putting his design into action, he went to see old Palemon and ask his advice.

He found him in his garden watering his lettuces. It was the evening. The blue Nile flowed at the foot of violet hills. The good old man was walking slowly, in order not to frighten a pigeon that had perched on his shoulder.

"The Lord be with thee, brother Paphnutius," he said. "Admire his goodness; He sends me the animals that He has created that I may converse with them of His works, and praise Him in the birds of the air. Look at this pigeon; note the changing hues of its neck, and say, is it not a beautiful work of God? But have you not come to talk with me, brother, on some pious subject? If so, I will put down my watering-pot, and listen to you."

Paphnutius told the old man about his journey, his return, the visions of his days and the dreams of his nights, — without omitting the sinful one — and the pack of jackals.

"Do you not think, father," he added, "that I ought to bury myself in the desert, and perform some extraordinary austerities that would even astonish the devil?"

"I am but a poor sinner," replied Palemon, "and I know little about men, having passed all my life in this garden, with gazelles, little hares and pigeons. But it seems to me, brother, that your distemper comes from your having passed too suddenly from the noisy world to the calm of solitude. Such sudden transitions can but do harm to the health of the soul. You are, brother, like a man who exposes himself, almost at the same time, to great heat and great cold. A cough shakes him, and fever torments him. In your place, brother Paphnutius, instead of retiring at once into some awful desert, I should take such amusements as are fitting to a monk and a holy abbot. I should visit the monasteries in the neighborhood. Some of them are wonderful, it is said. That of Abbot Serapion contains, I have been told, a thousand four hundred and thirty-two cells, and the monks are divided into as many legions as there are letters in the Greek alphabet. I am even informed that a certain analogy is observed between the character of the monks and the shape of the letter by which they are designated, and that, for example, those who are placed under Z have a tortuous character, whilst those under I have an upright mind. If I were you, brother,

I should go and assure myself of this with my own eyes, and I should know no rest until I had seen such a wonderful thing. I should not fail to study the regulations of the various communities which are scattered along the banks of the Nile, so as to be able to compare one with another. Such study is befitting a religious man like yourself. You have heard say, no doubt, that Abbot Ephrem has drawn up for his monastery pious regulations of great beauty. With his permission, you might make a copy of them, as you are a skilful penman. I could not do so, for my hands, accustomed to wield the spade, are too awkward to direct the thin reed of the scribe over the papyrus. But you have the knowledge of letters, brother, and should thank God for it, for beautiful writing cannot be too much admired. The work of the copyist and the reader is a great safeguard against evil thoughts. Brother Paphnutius, why do you not write out the teachings of our fathers, Paul and Anthony? Little by little you would recover, in these pious works, peace of soul and mind; solitude would again become pleasant to your heart, and soon you would be in a condition to recommence those ascetic works which your journey has interrupted. But you must not expect much benefit from excessive penitence. When he was amongst us, our Father Anthony used to say, 'Excessive fasting produces weakness, and weakness begets idleness. There are some monks who ruin their body by fasts improperly prolonged. Of them it may be said that they plunge a dagger into their own breast, and deliver themselves up unresistingly into the power of the devil.' So said the holy man, Anthony. I am but a foolish old man, but, by the grace of God, I have remembered what our father told us."

Paphnutius thanked Palemon and promised to think over his advice. When he had passed the fence of reeds which enclosed the little garden, he turned round and saw the good old gardener engaged in watering his salads, whilst the pigeon walked about on his bent back, and at that sight Paphnutius felt ready to weep.

On returning to his cell, he found there a strange turmoil, as though it were filled with grains of sand blown about by a strong wind, and on looking closer, he saw these moving bodies were myriads of little jackals. That night he saw in a dream, a high stone column surmounted by a human face, and he heard a voice which said —

"Ascend this pillar!"

On awaking, he felt confident that this dream had been sent from heaven. He called his disciples, and addressed them in these words —

"My beloved sons, I must leave you, and go where God sends me. During my absence obey Flavian as you would me, and take care of our brother Paul. Bless you. Farewell."

As he strode away, they remained prostrate on the ground, and when they raised their heads, they saw his tall dark figure on the sandy horizon.

He walked day and night until he reached the ruins of the temple, formerly built by the idolaters, in which he had slept amongst the scorpions and sirens on his former strange journey. The walls, covered with magic signs, were still standing. Thirty immense columns, which terminated in human heads or lotus flowers, still supported a heavy stone entablature. But, at one end of the temple, a pillar had shaken off its old burden, and stood isolated. It had for its capital the head of a woman which smiled, with long eyes and rounded cheeks, and on her forehead cow's horns.

Paphnutius, on seeing it, recognized the column which had been shown him in his dream, and he calculated that it was thirty-two cubits high. He went to the neighboring village, and ordered a ladder of that height to be made; and when the ladder was placed against the pillar, he ascended, knelt down on the top, and said to the Lord —

"Here, then, O God, is the abode Thou hast chosen for me. May I remain here, in Thy Grace, until the hour of my death."

He had brought no provisions with him, trusting in divine providence, and expecting that charitable peasants would give him all that he needed. And, in fact, the next day, about the ninth hour, women came with their children, bringing bread, dates, and fresh water, which the boys carried to the top of the column.

The top of the pillar was not large enough to allow the monk to lie at full length, so that he slept with his legs crossed and his head on his breast, and sleep was a more cruel torture to him than his wakeful hours. At dawn the ospreys brushed him with their wings, and he awoke filled with pain and terror.

It happened that the carpenter who had made the ladder feared God. Disturbed at the thought that the saint was exposed to the sun and rain, and fearing that he might fall in his sleep, this pious man constructed a roof and a railing on the top of the column.

Soon the report of this extraordinary existence spread from village to village, and the laborers of the valley came on Sundays, with their wives and children, to look at the stylite. The disciples of Paphnutius, having learned with surprise the place of this wonderful retreat, came to him, and obtained from him permission to build their huts at the foot of the column. Every morning they came and stood in a circle round the master, and received from him the words of instruction.

"My sons," he said to them, "continue like those little children whom Jesus loved. That is the way of salvation. The sin of the flesh is the source and origin of all sins; they spring from it as from a parent. Pride, avarice, idleness, anger, and envy are its dearly beloved progeny. I have seen this in Alexandria; I have seen rich men carried away by the vice of lust, which, like a river with a turbid flood, swept them into the gulf of bitterness."

The abbots Ephrem and Serapion, being informed of his strange proceeding, wished to behold him with their own eyes. Seeing from afar, on the river, the triangular sail which was bringing them to him, Paphnutius could not prevent himself from thinking that God had made him an example to all solitary monks. The two abbots, when they saw him, did not conceal their surprise; and, having consulted together, they agreed in condemning such an extraordinary penance, and exhorted Paphnutius to come down.

"Such a mode of life is contrary to all usage," they said; "it is peculiar, and against all rules."

But Paphnutius replied —

"What is the monastic life if not peculiar? And ought not the deeds of a monk to be as eccentric as he is himself? It was a sign from God that caused me to ascend here; it is a sign from God that will make me descend."

Every day religious men came to join the disciples of Paphnutius, and they built for themselves shelters round the aerial hermitage. Several of them, to imitate the saint, mounted the ruins of the temple; but, being reproved by their brethren, and conquered by fatigue, they soon gave up these attempts.

Pilgrims flocked from all parts. There were some who had come long distances, and were hungry and thirsty. The idea occurred to a poor widow of selling fresh water and melons. Against the foot of the column, behind her bottles of red clay, her cups and her fruit under an awning of blue-and-white striped canvas, she cried, "Who wants to drink?" Following the example of this widow, a baker brought some bricks and made an oven close by, in the hope of selling loaves and cakes to visitors. As the crowd of visitors increased unceasingly, and the inhabitants of the large cities of Egypt began to come, some man, greedy of gain, built a caravanserai to lodge the guests and their servants, camels, and mules. Soon there was, in front of the column, a market to which the fishermen of the Nile brought their fish, and the gardeners their vegetables. A barber, who shaved people in the open air, amused the crowd with his jokes. The old temple, so long given over to silence and solitude was filled with countless sights and sounds of life. The innkeepers turned the subterranean vaults into cellars and nailed on the old pillars signs surmounted by the figure of the holy Paphnutius, and bearing this inscription in Greek and Egyptian — *"Pomegranate wine, fig wine, and genuine Cilician beer sold here."* On the walls, sculptured with pure and graceful carvings, the shop-keepers hung ropes of onions, and smoked fish, dead hares, and the carcasses of sheep. In the evening, the old occupants of the ruins, the rats, scuttled in a long row to the river, whilst the ibises, suspiciously craning their necks, perched on the high cornices, to which rose the smoke of the kitchens, the shouts of the drinkers, and the cries of the tapsters. All around, builders laid out streets, and masons constructed convents, chapels, and churches. By the end of six months a city was established with a guardhouse, a tribunal, a prison, and a school, kept by an old blind scribe.

The pilgrims were innumerable. Bishops and other Church dignitaries, came, full of admiration. The Patriarch of Antioch, who chanced to be in Egypt at that time, came with all his clergy. He highly approved of the extraordinary conduct of the stylite, and the heads of the Libyan Church followed, in the absence of Athanasius, the opinion of the Patriarch. Having learned which, Abbots Ephrem and Serapion came to the feet of Paphnutius to apologize for their former mistrust. Paphnutius replied —

"Know, my brothers, that the penance I endure is barely equal to the temptations which are sent me, the number and force of which astound me. A man, viewed externally, is but small, and, from the height of the pillar to which God has called me, I see human beings moving about like ants. But, considered internally, man is immense; he is as large as the world, for he contains it. All that is spread before me — these monasteries, these inns, the boats on the river, the villages, and what I see in the distance of fields, canals, sand, and mountains — is nothing in respect to what is in me. I carry in my heart countless cities and illimitable deserts. And evil — evil and death — spread over this immensity, cover them all, as night covers the earth. I am, in myself alone, a universe of evil thoughts."

He spoke thus because the desire for woman was in him.

The seventh month, there came from Alexandria, Bubastis and Saï, women who had long been barren, hoping to obtain children by the intercession of the holy man and the virtues of his pillar. They rubbed their sterile bodies against the stone. There followed a procession, as far as the eye could reach, of chariots, palanquins, and litters, which stopped and pushed and jostled below the man of God. From them came sick people terrible to see. Mothers brought to Paphnutius young boys whose limbs were twisted, their eyes starting, their mouth foaming, their voices hoarse. He laid his hands upon them. Blind men approached, groping with their hands, and raising towards him a face pierced with two bleeding holes. Paralytics displayed before him the heavy immobility, the deadly emaciation, and the hideous contractions of their limbs; lame men showed him their club feet; women with cancer, holding their bosoms with both hands, uncovered before him their breasts devoured by the invisible vulture. Dropsical women, swollen like wine skins were placed on the ground before him. He blessed them. Nubians, afflicted with elephantiasis, advanced with heavy steps and looked at him with streaming eyes and expressionless countenances. He made the sign of the cross over them. A young girl of Aphroditopolis was brought to him on a litter; after having vomited blood, she had slept for three days. She looked like a waxen image, and her parents, who thought she was dead, had placed a palm leaf on her breast. Paphnutius having prayed to God, the young girl raised her head and opened her eyes.

As the people reported everywhere the miracles which the saint had performed, unfortunate persons afflicted with that disease which the Greeks call "the divine malady," came from all parts of Egypt in incalculable legions. As soon as they saw the pillar, they were seized with convulsions, rolled on the ground, writhed, and twisted themselves into a ball. And — though it is hardly to be believed — the persons present were in their turn seized with a violent delirium, and imitated the contortions of the epileptics. Monks and pilgrims, men and women, wallowed and struggled pell-mell, their limbs twisted, foaming at the mouth, eating handfuls of earth and prophesying. And Paphnutius at the top of his pillar felt a thrill of horror pass through him, and cried to God —

"I am the scapegoat, and I take upon me all the impurities of these people, and that is why, Lord, my body is filled with evil spirits."

Every time that a sick person went away healed, the people applauded, carried him in triumph, and ceased not to repeat —

"We behold another well of Siloam!"

Hundreds of crutches already hung round the wonderful column; grateful women suspended wreaths and votive images there. Some of the Greeks inscribed distiches, and as every pilgrim carved his name, the stone was soon covered as high as a man could reach with an infinity of Latin, Greek, Coptic, Punic, Hebrew, Syrian, and magic characters.

When the feast of Easter came there was such an affluence of people to this city of miracles that old men thought that the days of the ancient mysteries had returned. All sorts of people, in all sorts of costumes, were to be seen there; the striped robes of the Egyptians, the burnoose of the Arabs, the white drawers of the Nubians, the short cloak of the Greeks, the long toga of the Romans, the scarlet breeches of the barbarians, the gold-spangled robes of the courtesans. A veiled woman would pass on an ass, preceded by black eunuchs, who cleared a passage for her by the free use of their sticks. Acrobats, having spread a carpet on the ground, juggled and performed skilful tricks before a circle of silent spectators. Snake-charmers unrolled their living girdles. A glittering, dusty, noisy, chattering crowd! The curses of the camel-drivers beating the animals; the cries of the hawkers who sold amulets against leprosy and the evil eye; the psalmody of the monks reciting verses of the Bible; the shrieking of the women who were prophesying; the shouting of the beggars singing old songs of the harem; the bleating of sheep; the braying of asses; the sailors calling tardy passengers; all these confused noises caused a deafening uproar, over which dominated the strident voices of the little naked Negro boys, running about everywhere selling fresh dates.

And all these human beings stifled under the white sky, in a heavy atmosphere laden with the perfumes of women, the odor of Negroes, the fumes of cooking and the smoke of gums, which the devotees bought of the shepherds to burn before the saint.

When night came, fires, torches, and lanterns were lighted everywhere, and nothing was to be seen but red shadows and black shapes. Standing amidst a circle of squatting listeners, an old man, his face lighted by a smoky lamp, related how, formerly, Bitiou had enchanted his heart, torn it from his breast, placed it in an acacia, and then transformed himself into a tree. He made gestures, which his shadow repeated with absurd exaggerations, and the audience uttered cries of admiration. In the taverns. the drinkers. lying on couches, called for beer and wine. Dancing girls, with painted eyes and bare stomachs, performed before them religious or lascivious scenes. In retired corners, young men played dice or other games, and old men followed prostitutes. Above all these rose the solitary, unchanging column; the head with the cow's horns gazed into the shadow, and above it Paphnutius watched between heaven and earth. All at once the moon rose over the Nile, like the bare shoulder of a goddess. The hills gleamed with blue light, and Paphnutius thought he saw the body of Thaïs shinning in the glimmer of the waters amidst the sapphire night.

The days passed, and the saint still lived on his pillar. When the rainy season came, the waters of heaven, filtering through the cracks in the roof, wetted his body; his stiff limbs were incapable of movement. Scorched by the sun, and reddened by the dew, his skin broke; large ulcers devoured his arms and legs. But the desire of Thaïs still consumed him inwardly, and he cried —

"It is not enough, great God! More temptations! More unclean thoughts! More horrible desires! Lord, lay upon me all the lusts of men, that I may expiate them all! Though it is false that the Greek bitch took upon herself all the sins of the world, as I heard an impostor once declare, yet there is a hidden meaning in the fable, the truth of which I now recognize. For it is true that the sins of the people enter the soul of the saints, and are lost there as in a well. Thus it is that the souls of the just are polluted with more filth than is ever found in the soul of the sinner. And, for that reason, I praise Thee, O my God, for having made me the cesspool of the world."

One day, a rumor ran through the holy city, and even reached the ears of the hermit: a very great personage, a man occupying a high position, the Prefect of the Alexandrian fleet, Lucius Aurelius Cotta, was about to visit the city — was, indeed, now on his way.

The news was true. Old Cotta, who was inspecting the canals and the navigation of the Nile, had many times expressed a desire to see the stylite and the new city, to which the name of Stylopolis had been given. The Stylopolitans saw the river covered with sails one morning. Cotta appeared on board a golden galley hung with purple, and followed by all his fleet. He landed, and advanced, accompanied by a secretary carrying his tablets, and Aristæus, his physician, with whom he liked to converse.

A numerous suite walked behind him, and the shore was covered with *laticlaves** and military uniforms. He stopped, some paces from the column, and began to examine the stylite, wiping his face meanwhile with the skirt of his toga. Being of a naturally curious disposition, he had observed many things in the course of his long voyages. He liked to remember them, and intended to write, after he had finished his Punic history, a book on the remarkable things he had witnessed. He seemed much interested by the spectacle before him.

"This is very curious!" he said, puffing and blowing. "And — which is a circumstance worthy of being recorded — this man was my guest. Yes, this monk supped with me last year, after which he carried off an actress."

Turning to his secretary —

---

* The *laticlave* was a toga, with a broad purple band, worn by Roman senators as the distinguishing mark of their high office.

"Note that, my son, on my tablets; also the dimensions of the column, not omitting the shape of the top of it."

Then, wiping his face again —

"Persons deserving of belief have assured me that this monk has not left his column for a single moment since he mounted it a year ago. Is that possible, Aristæus?"

"That which is possible to a lunatic or a sick man," replied Aristæus, "would be impossible to a man sound in body and mind. Do you know, Lucius, that sometimes diseases of the mind or body give to those afflicted by them a strength which healthy men do not possess? For, as a matter of fact, there is no such thing as good health or bad health. There are only different conditions of the organs. Having studied what are called maladies, I have come to consider them as necessary forms of life. I take pleasure in studying them in order to be able to conquer them. Some of them are worthy of admiration, and conceal, under apparent disorder, profound harmonies; for instance, a quartan fever is certainly a very pretty thing! Sometimes certain affections of the body cause a rapid augmentation of the faculties of the mind. You know Creon? When he was a child, he stuttered and was stupid. But, having cracked his skull by tumbling off a ladder, he became an able lawyer, as you are aware. This monk must be affected in some hidden organ. Moreover, this kind of existence is not so extraordinary as it appears to you, Lucius. I may remind you that the gymnosophists of India can remain motionless, not merely for a year, but during twenty, thirty, or forty years."

"By Jupiter!" cried Cotta, "that is a strange madness. For man was born to move and act, and idleness is an unpardonable crime, because it is an injury to the State. I do not know of any religion in which such an objectionable practice is permitted, though it possibly may be in some of the Asiatic creeds. When I was Governor of Syria, I found *phalli* erected in the porches at the city of Hera. A man ascended, twice a year, and remained there for a week. The people believed that this man talked with the gods, and interceded with them for the prosperity of Syria. The custom appeared senseless to me; nevertheless I did nothing to put it down. For I consider that a functionary ought not to interfere with the manners and customs of the people, but on the contrary, to see that they are preserved. It is not the business of the government to force a religion on a people, but to maintain that which exists, which, whether good or bad, has been regulated by the spirit of the time, the place, and the race. If it endeavors to put down a religion, it proclaims itself revolutionary in its spirit, and tyrannical in its acts, and is justly detested. Besides, how are you to raise yourself above the superstitions of the vulgar, except by under-standing them and tolerating them? Aristsus, I am of opinion that I should leave this nephelo-coccygian* in the air, exposed only to the indignities the birds shower on him. I should not gain anything by having him pulled down, but I should by taking note of his thoughts and beliefs."

He puffed, coughed, and placed his hand on the secretary's shoulder.

"My child, note down that, amongst certain sects of Christians, it is considered praiseworthy to carry off courtesans and live upon columns. You may add that these customs are evidence of the worship of genetic divinities. But on this point we ought to question him himself."

Then, raising his head, and shading his eyes with his hand, to keep off the sun, he shouted —

"Hallo, Paphnutius! If you remember that you were

---

* Nephelo-coccygia, the cloud-city built by the cuckoos, in the *Birds* of Aristophanes.

once my guest, answer me. What are you doing up there? Why did you go up, and why do you stay there? Has this column any phallic signification in your mind?"

Paphnutius, considering Cotta as nothing but an idolater, did not deign to reply. But his disciple, Flavian, approached, and said —

"Illustrious Sir, this holy man takes the sins of the world upon him, and cures diseases."

"By Jupiter! Do you hear, Aristæus?" cried Cotta. "This nephelo- coccygian practices medicine, like you. What do you think of so high a rival?"

Aristæus shook his head.

"It is very possible that he may cure certain diseases better than I can; such, for instance, as epilepsy, vulgarly called the divine malady, although all maladies are equally divine, for they all come from the gods. But the cause of this disease lies, partly, in the imagination, and you must confess, Lucius, that this monk, perched up on the head of a goddess, strikes the minds of the sick people more forcibly than I, bending over my mortars and phials in my laboratory, could ever do. There are forces, Lucius, infinitely more powerful than reason and science."

"What are they?" asked Cotta.

"Ignorance and folly," replied Aristæus.

"I have rarely seen a more curious sight," continued Cotta, "and I hope that some day an able writer will relate the foundation of Stylopolis. But even the most extraordinary spectacles should not keep, longer than is befitting, a serious and busy man from his work. Let us go and inspect the canals. Farewell, good Paphnutius! or rather, till our next meeting! If ever you should come down to earth again, and revisit Alexandria, do not fail to come and sup with me."

These words, heard by all present, passed from mouth to mouth, and being repeated by the believers, added greatly to the reputation of Paphnutius. Pious minds amplified and transformed them, and it was stated that Paphnutius, from the top of his pillar, had converted the Prefect of the Fleet to the faith of the apostles and the Nicæan fathers. The believers found a figurative meaning in the last words uttered by Aurelius Cotta; to them, the supper to which this important personage had invited the ascetic, was a holy communion, a spiritual repast, a celestial banquet. The story of this meeting was embroidered with wonderful details, which those who invented were the first to believe. It was said that when Cotta, after a long argument, had embraced the truth, an angel had come from heaven to wipe the sweat from his brow. The physician and secretary of the Prefect of the Fleet had also, it was asserted, been converted at the same time. And, the miracle being public and notorious, the deacons of the principal churches of Libya recorded it amongst the authentic facts. After that, it could be said, without any exaggeration, that the whole world was seized with a desire to see Paphnutius, and that, in the West as well as the East, all Christians turned their astonished eyes towards him. The most celebrated cities of Italy sent deputations to him, and the Roman Cæsar, the divine Constantine who favored the Christian religion, wrote him a letter which the legates brought to him with great ceremony. But one night, whilst the budding city at his feet slept in the dew, he heard a voice, which said —

"Paphnutius, thou art become celebrated by thy works and powerful by thy word. God has raised thee up for His glory. He has chosen thee to work miracles, heal the sick, convert the Pagans, enlighten sinners, confound the Arians, and establish peace in the Church."

Paphnutius replied —

"God's will be done!"

The voice continued —

"Arise, Paphnutius, and go seek in his palace the impious Constans, who, far from imitating the wisdom of his brother, Constantine, inclines to the errors of Arius and Marcus. Go! The bronze gates shall fly open before thee, and thy sandals shall resound on the golden floor of the basilica before the throne of the Cæsars, and thy awe-inspiring voice shall change the heart of the son of Constantinus. Thou shalt reign over a peaceful and powerful Church. And, even as the soul directs the body, so shall the Church govern the empire. Thou shalt be placed above senators, comites, and patricians. Thou shalt repress the greed of the people, and check the boldness of the barbarians. Old Cotta, knowing that thou art the head of the government, will seek the honor of washing thy feet. At thy death thy *cilicium* shall be taken to the patriarch of Alexandria, and the great Athanasius, white with glory, shall kiss it as the relic of a saint. Go!"

Paphnutius replied —

"Let the will of God be accomplished!"

And making an effort to stand up, he prepared to descend. But the voice, divining his intention, said —

"Above all, descend not by the ladder. That would be to act like an ordinary man, and to be unconscious of the gifts that are in thee. A great saint, like thee, ought to fly through the air. Leap! the angels are there to support thee. Leap, then!"

Paphnutius replied —

"The will of God be done, on earth as it is in heaven."

Extending his long arms like the ragged wings of a huge sick bird, he was about to throw himself down, when, suddenly, a hideous mocking laugh rang in his ears. Terrified, he asked —

"Who laughs thus?"

"Ah? ah!" screamed the voice, "we are yet but at the beginning of our friendship; thou wilt some day be better acquainted with me. My friend, it was I who caused thee to ascend here, and I ought to be satisfied at the docility with which thou hast accomplished my wishes. Paphnutius, I am pleased with thee."

Paphnutius murmured, in a voice stifled by fear —

"Avaunt, avaunt! I know thee now; thou art he who carried Jesus to a pinnacle of the temple, and showed him all the kingdoms of this world."

He fell, affrighted, on the stone.

"Why did I not know this sooner?" he thought. "More wretched than the blind, deaf, and paralyzed who trust in me, I have lost all knowledge of things supernatural, and am more depraved than the maniacs who eat earth and approach dead bodies. I can no longer distinguish between the clamors of hell and the voices of heaven. I have lost even the intuition of the new-born child, who cries when its nurse's breast is taken from it, of the dog that scents out its master's footsteps, of the plant that turns towards the sun. I am the laughing-stock of the devils. So, then, it is Satan who led me here. When he elevated me on this pedestal, lust and pride mounted with me. It is not the magnitude of my temptations which terrifies me. Anthony, on his mountain, suffers the same. I wish that all their swords may pierce my flesh, before the eyes of the angels. I have even learned to like my sufferings. But God does not speak to me, and His silence astonishes me. He has left me — and I had but Him to look to. He leaves me alone in the horror of His absence. He flies from me. I will follow after Him. This stone burns my feet. Let me leave quickly, and come up with God."

With that he seized the ladder which stood against the column, put his feet on it, and having descended a rung, found himself face to face with the monster's head; she smiled strangely. He was certain then that what he had taken for the site of his rest and glory, was but the diabolical instrument of his trouble and damnation. He hastily descended and touched the soil. His feet had forgotten their use, and he reeled. But, feeling on him the shadow of the cursed column, he forced himself to run. All slept. He traversed, without being seen, the great square surrounded by wine-shops, inns, and caravanserais, and threw himself into a by-street which led towards the Libyan Hills. A dog pursued him, barking, and stopped only at the edge of the desert. Paphnutius went through a country where there was no road but the trail of wild beasts. Leaving behind him the huts abandoned by the coiners, he continued all night and all day his solitary flight.

At last, almost ready to expire with hunger, thirst, and fatigue, and not knowing if God was still far from him, he came to a silent city which extended from right to left, and stretched away till it was lost in the blue horizon. The buildings, which were widely separated and like each other, resembled pyramids cut off at half their height. They were tombs. The doors were broken, and in the shadow of the chambers could be seen the gleaming eyes of hyænas and wolves who brought forth their young there, whilst the dead bodies lay on the threshold, despoiled by robbers, and gnawed by the wild beasts. Having passed through this funeral city, Paphnutius fell exhausted before a tomb which stood near a spring surrounded by palm trees. This tomb was much ornamented, and, as there was no door to it, he saw inside it a painted chamber, in which serpents bred.

"Here," he sighed, "is the abode I have chosen; the tabernacle of my repentance and penitence."

He dragged himself to it, drove out the reptiles with his feet, and remained prostrate on the stone floor for eighteen hours, at the end of which time he went to the spring, and drank out of his hand. Then he plucked some dates and some stalks of lotus, the seeds of which he ate. Thinking this kind of life was good, he made it the rule of his existence. From morning to night he never lifted his forehead from the stone.

One day, whilst he was thus prostrated, he heard a voice which said —

"Look at these images, that thou mayest learn."

Then, raising his head, he saw, on the walls of the chamber, paintings which represented lively and domestic scenes. They were of very old work, and marvelously lifelike. There were cooks who blew the fire, with their cheeks all puffed out; others plucked geese, or cooked quarters of sheep in stew-pans. A little farther, a hunter carried on his shoulders a gazelle pierced with arrows. In one place, peasants were sowing, reaping, or gathering. In another, women danced to the sounds of viols, flutes, and harp. A young girl played the theorbo. The lotus flower shone in her hair, which was neatly braided. Her transparent dress let the pure forms of her body be seen. Her bosom and mouth were perfect. The face was turned in profile, and the beautiful eye looked straight before her. The whole figure was exquisite. Paphnutius having examined it, lowered his eyes, and replied to the voice —

"Why dost thou command me to look at these images? No doubt they represent the terrestrial life of the idolater whose body rests here, under my feet, at the bottom of a well, in a coffin of black basalt. They recall the life of a dead man, and are, despite their bright colors, the shadows of a shadow. The life of a dead man! O vanity!"

"He is dead, but he lived," replied the voice; "and thou wilt die, and wilt not have lived."

From that day, Paphnutius had not a moment's rest. The voice spoke to him incessantly. The girl with the theorbo looked fixedly at him from underneath the long lashes of her eye. At last she also spoke —

"Look. I am mysterious and beautiful. Love me. Exhaust in my arms the love which torments you. What use is it to fear me? You cannot escape me; I am the beauty of woman. Whither do you think to fly from me, senseless fool? You will find my likeness in the radiancy of flowers, and in the grace of the palm trees, in the flight of pigeons, in the bounds of the gazelle, in the rippling of brooks, in the soft light of the moon, and if you close your eyes, you will find me within yourself. It is a thousand years since the man who sleeps here, swathed in linen, in a bed of black stone, pressed me to his heart. It is a thousand years since he received the last kiss from my mouth, and his sleep is yet redolent with it. You know me well, Paphnutius. How is it you have not recognized me? I am one of the innumerable incarnations of Thaïs. You are a learned monk, and well skilled in the knowledge of things. You have traveled, and it is by travel a man learns the most. Often a day passed abroad will show more novelties than ten years passed at home. You have heard that Thaïs lived formerly in Argos, under the name of Helen. She had another existence in Thebes Hecatompyle. And I was Thaïs of Thebes. How is it you have not guessed it? I took, when I was alive, a large share in the sins of this world, and now reduced here to the condition of a shadow, I am still quite capable of taking your sins upon me, beloved monk. Whence comes your surprise? It was certain that, wherever you went, you would find Thaïs again."

He struck his forehead against the pavement, and uttered a cry of terror. And every night the player of the theorbo left the wall, approached him, and spoke in a clear voice mingled with soft breathing. And as the holy man resisted the temptations she gave him, she said to him —

"Love me; yield, friend. As long as you resist me I shall torment you. You do not know what the patience of a dead woman is. I shall wait, if necessary, till you are dead. Being a sorceress, I shall put into your lifeless body a spirit who will reanimate it, and who will not refuse me what I have asked in vain of you. And think, Paphnutius, what a strange situation when your blessed soul sees, from the height of heaven, its own body given up to sin. God, who has promised to return you this body after the day of judgment and the end of time, will Himself be much puzzled. How can He place in celestial glory a human form inhabited by a devil, and guarded by a sorceress? You have not thought of that difficulty. Nor God either, perhaps. Between ourselves, He is not very knowing. Any ordinary magician can easily deceive Him, and if He had not His thunder, and the cataracts of heaven, the village urchins would pull His beard. He has certainly not as much sense as the old serpent, His adversary. *He*, indeed, is a wonderful artist. If I am so beautiful, it is because he adorned me with all my attractions. It was he who taught me how to braid my hair, and to make for myself rosy fingers with agate nails. You have misunderstood him. When you came to live in this tomb, you drove out with your feet the serpents which were here, without troubling yourself to know whether they were of his family, and you crushed their eggs. I am afraid, my poor friend, you will have a troublesome business on your hands. You were warned, however, that he was a musician and a lover. What have you done? You have quarreled with science and beauty. You are altogether miserable, and Iaveh does not come to your help. It is not probable that he will come. Being as great as all things, he cannot move for want of space, and if, by an impossibility, he made the least movement, all creation would be pushed out of place. My handsome hermit, give me a kiss."

Paphnutius was aware that great prodigies are performed by magic arts. He thought — not without much uneasiness —

"Perhaps the dead man buried at my feet knows the words written in that mysterious book which exists hidden, not far from here, at the bottom of a royal tomb. By virtue of these words, the dead, taking the form which they had upon earth, see the light of the sun and the smiles of women."

His chief fear was that the girl with the theorbo and the dead man might come together, as they did in their lifetime, and that he should see them unite. Sometimes he thought he heard the sound of kissing.

He was troubled in his mind, and now, in the absence of God he feared to think as much as to feel. One evening, when he was kneeling prostrate according to his custom, an unknown voice said to him —

"Paphnutius, there are on earth more people than you imagine, and if I were to show you what I have seen, you would die of astonishment. There are men with a single eye in the middle of their forehead. There are men who have but one leg, and advance by jumps. There are men who change their sex, and the females become males. There are men-trees, who shoot out roots in the ground. And there are men with no head, with two eyes, a nose, and a mouth in their breast. Can you honestly believe that Jesus Christ died for the salvation of these men?"

Another time he had a vision. He saw, in a strong light, a broad road, rivulets, and gardens. On the road, Aristobulus and Chereas passed at a gallop on their Syrian horses, and the joyous ardor of the race reddened the cheeks of the two young men. Beneath a portico, Callicrates recited his verses; satisfied pride trembled in his voice and shone in his eyes. In the garden, Zenothemis picked apples of gold, and caressed a serpent with azure wings. Clad in white, and wearing a shining miter, Hermodorus meditated beneath a sacred persea, which bore, instead of flowers, small heads of pure profile, wearing, like the Egyptian goddesses, vultures, hawks, or the shining disk of the moon; whilst in the background, by the side of a fountain, Nicias studied, on an armillary sphere, the harmonious movements of the stars.

Then a veiled woman approached the monk, holding in her hand a branch of myrtle. She said to him —

"Look! Some seek eternal beauty, and place their ephemeral life in the infinite. Others live without much thought. But by that alone they submit to fair Nature, and they are happy and beautiful in the joy of living only, and give glory to the supreme artist of all things; for man is a noble hymn to God. All think that happiness is innocent, and that pleasure is permitted to man. Paphnutius, if they are right, what a dupe you have been!"

And the vision vanished.

Thus was Paphnutius tempted unceasingly in body and mind. Satan never gave him a minute's repose. The solitude of the tomb was more peopled than the streets of a great city. The devils shouted with laughter, and millions of imps, evil genii, and phantoms imitated all the ordinary transactions of life. In the evening, when he went to the spring, satyrs and nymphs capered round him, and tried to drag him into their lascivious dances. The demons no longer feared him. They loaded him with insults, obscene jests, and blows. One day a devil, no longer than his arm, stole the cord he wore round his waist.

He said to himself —

"Thought, whither hast thou led me?"

And he resolved to work with his hands, in order to give his mind that rest of which it had need. Near the spring, some banana trees, with large leaves, grew under the shade of the palms. He cut the stalks, and carried them to the tomb. He crushed them with a stone, and reduced them to fibers, as he had seen rope makers do. For he intended to make a cord, to replace that which the devil had stolen. The demons were somewhat displeased at this; they ceased their clamor, and the girl with the theorbo no longer continued her magic arts, but remained quietly on the wall. The courage and faith of Paphnutius increased whilst he pounded the banana stems.

"With Heaven's help," he said to himself, "I shall subdue the flesh. As to my soul, its confidence is still unshaken. In vain do the devils, and that accursed woman, try to instill into my mind doubts as to the nature of God. I will reply to them, by the mouth of the Apostle John, 'In the beginning was the Word, and the Word was God.' That I firmly believe, and that which I believe is absurd, I believe still more firmly. In fact it should be absurd. If it were not so, I should not believe; I should know. And it is not that which we know which gives eternal life; it is faith only that saves."

He exposed the separated fibers to the sun and the dew, and every morning he took care to turn them, to prevent them rotting; and he rejoiced to find that he had become as simple as a child. When he had twisted his cord, he cut reeds to make mats and baskets. The sepulchral chamber resembled a basket-maker's work-shop, and Paphnutius could pass without difficulty from work to prayer. Yet still God was not merciful to him, for one night he was awakened by a voice which froze him with horror, for he guessed that it was the voice of the dead man.

The voice called quickly, in a light whisper —

"Helen! Helen! come and bathe with me! come quickly!"

A woman, whose mouth was close to the monk's ear, replied —

"Friend, I cannot rise; a man is lying on me."

Paphnutius suddenly perceived that his cheek rested on a woman's breast. He recognized the player of the theorbo, who, partly relieved of his weight, raised her breast. He clung tightly to the sweet, warm, perfumed body, and consumed with the desire of damnation, he cried —

"Stay, stay, my heavenly one!"

But she was already standing on the threshold. She laughed, and her smile gleamed in the silver rays of the moon.

"Why should I stay?" she said. "The shadow of a shadow is enough for a lover endowed with such a lively imagination. Besides, you have sinned. What more was needed?"

Paphnutius wept in the night, and when the dawn came, he murmured a prayer that was a meek complaint —

"Jesus, my Jesus, why hast Thou forsaken me! Thou seest the danger in which I am. Come, and help me, sweet Savior. Since Thy Father no longer loves me, and does not hear me, remember that I have but Thee. From Him nothing is to be hoped; I cannot comprehend Him, and He cannot pity me. But Thou was born of a woman, and that is why I trust in Thee. Remember that Thou wast a man. I pray to Thee, not because Thou art God of God, Light of light, very God of very God, but because Thou hast lived poor and humble on this earth where now I suffer, because Satan has tempted Thy flesh, because the sweat of agony has bedewed Thy face. It is to Thy humanity that I pray, Jesus, my brother Jesus!"

When he had thus prayed, wringing his hands, a terrible peal of laughter shook the walls of the tomb, and the voice which rang in his ears on the top of the column, said jeeringly —

"That is a prayer worthy of the breviary of Marcus, the heretic. Paphnutius is an Arian! Paphnutius is an Arian!"

As though thunderstruck, the monk fell senseless.

*W*hen he reopened his eyes, he saw around him monks wearing black hoods, who poured water on his temples, and recited exorcisms. Many others were standing outside, carrying palm leaves.

"As we passed through the desert," said one of them, "we heard cries issuing from this tomb, and, having entered, we found you lying unconscious on the floor. Doubtless the devils had thrown you down, and had fled at our approach."

Paphnutius, raising his head, asked in a feeble voice —

"Who are you, my brothers? And why do you carry palms in your hands? Is it for my burial?"

One of them replied —

"Brother, do you not know that our father, Anthony, now a hundred and five years old, having been warned of his approaching end, has come down from Mount Colzin, to which he had retired, to bless his numerous spiritual children? We are going with palm leaves to greet our holy father. But how is it, brother, that you are ignorant of such a great event? Can it be possible that no angel came to this tomb to inform you?"

"Alas!" replied Paphnutius, "I am not worthy of such a favor, and the only denizens of this abode are demons and vampires. Pray for me. I am Paphnutius, Abbot of Antinoë, the most wretched of the servants of God."

At the name of Paphnutius, all waved their palm leaves and murmured his praises. The monk who had previously spoken, cried in surprise —

"Can it be that thou art that holy Paphnutius, celebrated for so many works that it was supposed he would some day equal the great Anthony himself? Most venerable, it was thou who convertedst to God the courtesan, Thaïs, and who, raised upon a high column, was carried away by the seraphs. Those who watched by night, at the foot of the pillar, saw thy blessed assumption. The wings of the angels encircled thee in a white cloud, and with thy right hand extended thou didst bless the dwellings of man. The next day, when the people saw thou wert no longer there, a long groan rose to the summit of the discrowned pillar. But Flavian, thy disciple, reported the miracle, and took thy place as the head. But a foolish man, of the name of Paul, tried to contradict the general opinion. He asserted that he had seen thee, in a dream, carried away by the devils; the people wanted to stone him, and it was a miracle that he escaped death. I am Zozimus, abbot of these solitary monks whom thou seest prostrate at thy feet. Like them, I kneel before thee, that thou mayest bless the father with the children. Then thou shalt relate to us the marvels which God has deigned to accomplish by thy means."

"Far from having favored me as thou believest," replied Paphnutius, "the Lord has tried me with terrible temptations. I was not carried away by angels. But a shadowy wall is raised in front of my eyes, and moves before me. I have lived in a dream. Without God all is a dream. When I made my journey to Alexandria, I heard, in a short space of time, many discourses, and I learned that the army of errors was innumerable. It pursues me, and I am compassed about with swords."

Zozimus replied –

"Venerable father, we must remember that the saints, and especially the solitary saints, undergo terrible trials. If thou wast not carried to heaven by the seraphs, it is certain that the Lord granted that favor to thy image, for Flavian, the monks, and the people were witnesses of thy assumption."

Paphnutius resolved to go and receive the blessing of Anthony.

"Brother Zozimus," he said, "give me one of these palm leaves, and let us go and meet our father."

"Let us go," replied Zozimus; "military order is most

befitting for monks, who are God's soldiers. Thou and I, being abbots, will march in front, and the others shall follow us, singing psalms."

They set out on their march, and Paphnutius said —

"God is unity, for He is the truth, which is one. The world is many, because it is error. We should turn away from all the sights of nature, even those which appear the most innocent. Their diversity renders them pleasant, which is a sign that they are evil. For that reason, I cannot see a tuft of papyrus by the side of still waters without my soul being imbued with melancholy. All things that the senses perceive are detestable. The least grain of sand brings danger. Everything tempts us. Woman is but a combination of all the temptations scattered in the thin air, on the flowering earth, in the clear waters. Happy is he whose soul is a sealed vase! Happy is he who knows how to be deaf, dumb, and blind, and who knows nothing of the world, in order that he may know God!"

Zozimus, having meditated upon these words, replied as follows —

"Venerable father, it is fitting that I should avow my sins to thee, since thou hast shown me thy soul. Thus we shall confess to each other, according to the apostolic custom. Before I was a monk, I led an abominable life. At Madaura, a city celebrated for its courtesans, I sought out all kinds of worldly love. Every night I supped in company with young debauchees and female flute players, and I took home with me the one who pleased me the best. A saint like thee could never imagine to what a pitch the fury of my desires carried me. Suffice it to say that it spared neither matrons nor nuns, and spread adultery and sacrilege everywhere. I excited my senses with wine, and was justly known as the heaviest drinker in Madaura. Yet I was a Christian, and, in all my follies, kept my faith in Jesus crucified. Having devoured my substance in riotous living, I was beginning to feel the first attacks of poverty, when I saw one of my companions in pleasure suddenly struck with a terrible disease. His knees could not sustain him; his twitching hands refused to obey him; his glazed eyes closed. Only horrible groans came from his breast. His mind, heavier than his body, slumbered. To punish him for having lived like a beast, God had changed him into a beast. The loss of my property had already inspired me with salutary reflections, but the example of my friend was of yet greater efficacy; it made such an impression on my heart that I quitted the world and retired into the desert. There I have enjoyed for twenty years a peace that nothing has troubled. I work with my monks as weaver, architect, carpenter, and even as scribe, though, to say the truth, I have little taste for writing, having always preferred action to thought. My days are full of joy, and my nights without dreams, and I believe that the grace of the Lord is in me, because, even in the midst of the most frightful sins, I have never lost hope."

On hearing these words, Paphnutius lifted his eyes to heaven and murmured —

"Lord, Thou lookest with kindness upon this man polluted by adultery, sacrilege, and so many crimes, and Thou turnest away from me, who have always kept Thy commandments! How inscrutable is Thy justice, O my God! and how impenetrable are Thy ways!"

Zozimus extended his arms.

"Look, venerable father! On both sides of the horizon are long, black files that look like emigrant ants. They are our brothers, who, like us, are going to meet Anthony."

When they came to the place of meeting, they saw a magnificent spectacle. The army of monks extended, in three ranks, in an immense semicircle. In the first rank stood the old hermits of the desert, cross in hand, and with long beards that almost touched the ground.

The monks, governed by the abbots Ephrem and Serapion, and also all the cenobites of the Nile, formed the second line. Behind them appeared the ascetics, who had come from their distant rocks. Some wore, on their blackened and dried-up bodies, shapeless rags; others had for their only clothes, bundles of reeds held together by withies. Many of them were naked, but God had covered them with a fell of hair as thick as a sheep's fleece. All held branches of palm; they looked like an emerald rainbow, or they might have been also compared to the host of the elect — the living walls of the city of God.

Such perfect order reigned in the assembly, that Paphnutius found, without difficulty, the monks he governed. He placed himself near them, after having taken care to hide his face under his hood, that he might remain unknown, and not disturb them in their pious expectation. Suddenly, an immense shout arose —

"The saint!" they all cried. "The saint! Behold the great saint, against whom hell has not prevailed, the well-beloved of God! Our father, Anthony!"

Then a great silence followed, and every forehead was lowered to the sand.

From the summit of a dune, in the vast void space, Anthony advanced, supported by his beloved disciples, Macarius and Amathas. He walked slowly, but his figure was still upright, and showed the remains of a superhuman strength. His white beard spread over his broad chest, his polished skull reflected the rays of sunlight like the forehead of Moses. The keen gaze of the eagle was in his eyes; the smile of a child shone on his round cheek. To bless his people, he raised his arms, tired by a century of marvelous works, and his voice burst forth for the last time, with the words of love.

"How goodly are thy tents, O Jacob, and thy tabernacles, O Israel!"

Immediately, from one end to the other of the living wall, like a peal of harmonious thunder, the psalm, "Blessed is the man that feareth the Lord," broke forth.

Accompanied by Macarius and Amathas, Anthony passed along the ranks of the old hermits, anchorites, and cenobites. This seer, who had beheld heaven and hell; this hermit, who from a cave in the rock, governed the Christian Church; this saint, who had sustained the faith of the martyrs; this scholar, whose eloquence had paralyzed the heretics, spoke tenderly to each of his sons, and bade them a kindly farewell, on the eve of the blessed death, which God, who loved him, had at last promised him.

He said to the abbots Ephrem and Serapion —

"You command large armies, and you are both great generals. Therefore, you shall put on in heaven an armor of gold, and the Archangel Michael shall give you the title of kiliarchs of his hosts."

Perceiving the old man Philemon, he embraced him, and said —

"Behold, the kindest and best of all my children. His soul exhales a perfume as sweet as the flower of the beans he sows every year."

To Abbot Zozimus he addressed these words —

"Thou hast never mistrusted divine goodness, and therefore the peace of the Lord is in thee. The lily of thy virtues has flowered upon the dunghill of thy corruption."

To all he spoke words of unerring wisdom.

To the old hermits he said —

"The apostle saw, round the throne of God, eighty old men seated, clad in white robes, and wearing crowns on their heads."

To the young men —

"Be joyful; leave sadness to the happy ones of this world."

Thus he passed along the front of his filial army,

exhorting and comforting. Paphnutius, seeing him approach, fell on his knees, his heart torn by fear and hope.

"My father! my father!" he cried in his agony. "My father! come to my help, for I perish. I have given to God the soul of Thaïs; I have lived upon the top of a column, and in the chamber of a tomb. My forehead, unceasingly in the dust, has become horny as a camel's knee. And yet God has gone from me. Bless me, my father, and I shall be saved; shake the hyssop, and I shall be washed, and I shall shine as the snow."

Anthony did not reply. He turned to the monks of Antinoë those eyes whose looks no man could sustain. He gazed for a long time at Paul, called the Fool; then he made a sign to him to approach. And, as all were astonished that the saint should address himself to a man who was not in his senses, Anthony said —

"God has granted to him more grace than to any of you. Lift thy eyes, my son Paul, and tell me what thou seest in heaven."

Paul the Fool raised his eyes; his face shone, and his tongue was unloosed.

"I see in heaven," he said, "a bed adorned with hangings of purple and gold. Around it three virgins keep constant watch that no soul may approach it, except the chosen one for whom the bed is prepared."

Believing that this bed was the symbol of his glorification, Paphnutius had already begun to return thanks to God. But Anthony made a sign to him to be silent, and to listen to the Fool, who murmured in his ecstasy —

"The three virgins speak to me; they say unto me: 'A saint is about to quit the earth; Thaïs of Alexandria is dying. And we have prepared the bed of her glory, for we are her virtues — Faith, Fear, and Love.'"

Anthony asked —

"Sweet child, what else seest thou?"

Paul gazed vacantly from the zenith to the nadir, and from west to east, when suddenly his eyes fell on the Abbot of Antinoë. His face grew pale with a holy terror, and his eyeballs reflected invisible flames.

"I see," he murmured. "three demons, who, full of joy, prepare to seize that man. One of them is like unto a tower, one to a woman, and one to a mage. All three bear their name, marked with red-hot iron; the first on the forehead, the second on the belly, the third on the breast, and those names are — Pride, Lust, and Doubt. I have finished."

Having spoken thus, Paul, with haggard eyes and hanging jaw, returned to his old simple ways.

And, as the monks of Antinoë looked anxiously at Anthony, the saint pronounced these words —

"God has made known His just judgment. Let us bow to Him and hold our peace."

He passed. He bestowed blessings as he went. The sun, now descended to the horizon, enveloped him in its glory, and his shadow, immeasurably elongated by a miracle from heaven, unrolled itself behind him like an endless carpet, as a sign of the long remembrance this great saint would leave amongst men.

Upright, but thunderstruck, Paphnutius saw and heard nothing more. One word alone rang in his ears, "Thaïs is dying!" The thought had never occurred to him. Twenty years had he contemplated a mummy's head, and yet the idea that death would close the eyes of Thaïs astonished him hopelessly.

"Thaïs is dying!" An incomprehensible saying! "Thaïs is dying!" In those three words what a new and terrible sense! "Thaïs is dying!" Then why the sun, the flowers, the brooks, and all creation? "Thaïs is dying!" What good was all the universe? Suddenly he sprang forward. "To see her again, to see her once more!" He began to run. He knew not where he was, or whither he went, but instinct conducted him with unerring certainty; he went straight to the Nile. A swarm of sails covered the upper waters of the river. He sprang on board a barque manned by Nubians, and lying in the forepart of the boat, his eyes devouring space, he cried, in grief and rage —

"Fool, fool, that I was, not to have possessed Thaïs whilst there was yet time! Fool to have believed that there was anything else in the world but her! Oh, madness! I dreamed of God, of the salvation of my soul, of life eternal — as if all that counted for anything when I had seen Thaïs! Why did I not feel that blessed eternity was in a single kiss of that woman, and that without her life was senseless, and no more than an evil dream? Oh, stupid fool! thou hast seen her, and thou hast desired the good things of the other world! Oh, coward! thou hast seen her, and thou hast feared God! God! heaven! what are they? And what have they to offer thee which are worth the least tittle of that which she would have given thee? Oh, miserable, sense-less fool, who sought divine goodness elsewhere than on the lips of Thaïs! What hand was upon thy eyes? Cursed be he who blinded thee then! Thou couldst have bought, at the price of thy damnation, one mo-ment of her love, and thou hast not done it! She opened to thee her arms — flesh mingled with the perfume of flowers — and thou wast not engulfed in the unspeakable enchantments of her unveiled breast. Thou hast listened to the jealous voice which said to thee, 'Refrain!' Dupe, dupe, miserable dupe! Oh, re-grets! Oh, remorse! Oh, despair! Not to have the joy to carry to hell the memory of that never-to-be-forgot-ten hour, and to cry to God, 'Burn my flesh, dry up all the blood in my veins, break all my bones, thou canst not take from me the remembrance which sweet-ens and refreshes me for ever and ever!' . . . Thaïs is dying! Preposterous God, if thou knewest how I laugh at Thy hell! Thaïs is dying, and she will never be mine

— never! never!"

And as the boat came down the river with the current, he remained whole days lying on his face, and repeating —

"Never! never! never!"

Then, at the idea that she had given herself to others, and not to him; that she had poured forth an ocean of love, and he had not wetted his lips therein, he stood up, savagely wild, and howled with grief. He tore his breast with his nails, and bit the flesh of his arms. He thought —

"If I could but kill all those she has loved!"

The idea of these murders filled him with delicious fury. He dreamed of killing Nicias slowly and leisurely, looking him full in the eyes whilst he murdered him. Then suddenly his fury melted away. He wept, he sobbed. He became feeble and meek. An unknown tenderness softened his soul. He longed to throw his arms round the neck of the companion of his childhood and say to him, "Nicias, I love thee, because thou hast loved her. Talk to me about her. Tell me what she said to thee." And still, without ceasing, the iron of that phrase entered into his soul — "Thaïs is dying!"

"Light of day, silvery shadows of night stars, heavens, trees with trembling crests, savage beasts, domestic animals, all the anxious souls of men, do you not hear? 'Thaïs is dying!' Disappear, ye lights, breezes, and perfumes! Hide yourselves, ye shapes and thoughts of the universe! 'Thaïs is dying!' She was the beauty of the world, and all that drew near to her grew fairer in the reflection of her grace. The old man and the sages who sat near her, at the banquet at Alexandria, how pleasant they were, and how fascinating was their conversation! A host of brilliant thoughts sprang to their lips, and all their ideas were steeped in pleasure. And it was because the breath of Thaïs was on them that all they said was love, beauty, truth. A delightful impiety lent its grace to their discourse. They thoroughly expressed all human splendor. Alas! all that is but a dream. Thaïs is dying! Oh, how easy it will be to me to die of her death! But canst thou only die, withered embryo, fetus steeped in gall and scalding tears? Miserable abortion, dost thou think thou canst taste death, thou who hast never known life? If only God exists, that he may damn me. I hope for it — I wish it. God, I hate Thee — dost Thou hear? Overwhelm me with Thy damnation. To compel Thee to, I spit in Thy face. I must find an eternal hell, to exhaust the eternity of rage which consumes me."

*T*he next day, at dawn, Albina received the Abbot of Antinoë at the nunnery.

"Thou art welcome to our tabernacles of peace, venerable father, for no doubt, thou comest to bless the saint thou hast given us. Thou knowest that God, in his mercy, has called her to Him; how couldst thou fail to know tidings that the angels have carried from desert to desert? It is true that Thaïs is about to meet her blessed death. Her labors are accomplished, and I ought to inform thee, in a few words, as to her conduct whilst she was still amongst us. After thy departure, when she was confined in a cell sealed with thy seal, I sent her, with her food, a flute, similar to those which girls of her profession play at banquets. I did that to prevent her from falling into a melancholy mood, and that she should not show less skill and talent before God than she had shown before men. In this I showed prudence and foresight, for all day long Thaïs praised the Lord upon the flute, and the virgins, who were attracted by the sound of this invisible flute, said, 'We hear the nightingale of the heavenly groves, the dying

swan of Jesus crucified.' Thus did Thaïs perform her
penance, when, after sixty days, the door which thou
hadst sealed opened of itself, and the clay seal was
broken without being touched by any human hand.
By that sign I knew that the trial thou hadst imposed
upon her was at an end, and that God had pardoned
the sins of the flute-player. From that time she has
shared the ordinary life of my nuns, working and
praying with them. She was an example to them by the
modesty of her acts and words, and seemed like a statue
of purity amongst them. Sometimes she was sad; but
those clouds soon passed. When I saw that she was
really drawn towards God by faith, hope, and love, I
did not hesitate to employ her talent, and even her
beauty, for the improvement of her sisters. I asked her
to represent before us the actions of the famous women
and wise virgins of the Scriptures. She acted Esther,
Deborah, Judith, Mary, the sister of Lazarus, and Mary,
the mother of Jesus. I know, venerable father, that thy
austere mind is alarmed at the idea of these perform-
ances. But thou thyself wouldest have been touched if
thou hadst seen her in these pious scenes, shedding
real tears, and raising to heaven arms graceful as palm
leaves. I have long governed a community of women,
and I make it a rule never to oppose their nature. All
seeds give not the same flowers. Not all souls are
sanctified in the same way. It must also not be forgotten that Thaïs gave herself to God whilst she was still
beautiful, and such a sacrifice is, if not unexampled,
at least very rare. This beauty — her natural vesture —
has not left her during the three months' fever of which
she is dying. As, during her illness, she has incessantly
asked to see the sky, I have her carried every morning
into the courtyard, near the well, under the old fig tree,
in the shade of which the abbesses of this convent are
accustomed to hold their meetings. Thou wilt find her
there, venerable father; but hasten, for God calls her,

and this night a shroud will cover that face which God made both to shame and to edify this world."

Paphnutius followed her into a courtyard flooded with the morning light. On the edge of the brick roofs, the pigeons formed a string of pearls. On a bed, in the shade of the fig tree, Thaïs lay quite white, her arms crossed. By her side stood veiled women, reciting the prayers for the dying.

"Have mercy, upon me, O God, according to Thy loving kindness: according unto the multitude of Thy tender mercies blot out my transgressions."

He called her —

"Thaïs!"

She raised her eyelids, and turned the whites of her eyes in the direction of the voice.

Albina made a sign to the veiled women to retire a few paces.

"Thaïs!" repeated the monk.

She raised her head; a light breath came from her pale lips.

"Is it thou, my father? . . . Dost thou remember the water of the spring, and the dates that we picked? . . . That day, my father, love was born in my heart — the love of life eternal."

She was silent, and her head fell back.

Death was upon her, and the sweat of the last agony bedewed her forehead. A pigeon broke the still silence with its plaintive cooing. Then the sobs of the monk mingled with the psalms of the virgins.

"Wash me thoroughly from mine iniquity, and cleanse me from my sin. For I acknowledge my transgressions: and my sin is ever before me."

Suddenly Thaïs sat up in the bed. Her violet eyes opened wide, and with a rapt gaze, her arms stretched towards the distant hills, she said in a clear, fresh voice —

"Behold them — the roses of the eternal dawn!"

Her eyes shone; a slight flush suffused her face. She had revived, more sweet and more beautiful than ever. Paphnutius knelt down, and threw his long black arms around her.

"Do not die!" he cried, in a strange voice, which he himself did not recognize. "I love thee! Do not die! Listen, my Thaïs. I have deceived thee? I was but a wretched fool. God, heaven — all that is nothing. There is nothing true but this worldly life, and the love of human beings. I love thee! Do not die! That would be impossible — thou art too precious! Come, come with me! Let us fly? I will carry thee far away in my arms. Come, let us love! Hear me, O my beloved, and say, 'I will live; I wish to live.' Thaïs, Thaïs, arise!"

She did not hear him. Her eyes gazed into infinity. She murmured —

"Heaven opens. I see the angels, the prophets, and the saints. . . . The good Theodore is amongst them, his hands filled with flowers; he smiles on me and calls me. . . . Two angels come to me. They draw near. . . . How beautiful they are! I see God!"

She uttered a joyful sigh, and her head fell back motionless on the pillow. Thaïs was dead.

Paphnutius held her in a last despairing embrace; his eyes devoured her with desire, rage, and love.

Albina cried to him —

"Avaunt, accursed wretch!"

And she gently placed her fingers on the eyelids of the dead girl. Paphnutius staggered back, his eyes burning with flames and feeling the earth open beneath his feet.

The virgins chanted the song of Zacharias:

"Blessed be the Lord God of Israel."

Suddenly their voices stayed in their throat. They had seen the monk's face, and they fled in affright, crying —

"A vampire! A vampire!"

He had become so repulsive, that passing his hand over his face, he felt his own hideousness.

CPSIA information can be obtained
at www.ICGtesting.com
Printed in the USA
LVHW111124090619
620620LV00001B/308/P

9 781587 158551